MW00931008

The Long Road Ahead: The Turning

By Thomas Key

The Long Road Ahead: The Turning

By Thomas Key

Self-Published

Prologue

Rachel lay in her tan military issue cot with her soon-to-be husband beside her. The man next to her was Shepherd, a man who had been, quite literally, her knight in shining armor. A gang known as the Exiles had maintained a compound on the outskirts of Tucumcari, New Mexico. The vile men (for lack of a better term) took it upon themselves to be judge, jury, and executioners. Anyone they captured either joined their group, became slaves or were crucified in a macabre facsimile of the crucifixion of Christ. She had joined on last-minute onto a scouting mission from Cannon Air Force Base, joining a small crew with the goal of flying over a wide area of the base and checking for anything out of the ordinary. Her helicopter, however, an Air Force Black Hawk, had been tampered with. Insurgents had sabotaged many of the based air assets. Not long after takeoff, their bird went down, hitting the ground hard several miles from Tucumcari. It wasn't long before the event caused a welcome party to arrive. The Exiles were not gracious hosts by any stretch, and she was soon thrown into an old animal transportation trailer of some kind. Somehow, Shepherd, the man next to her; who had previously been missing and presumed dead in Albuquerque saved the day. Sneaking into the base under the cover of night, bypassing the perimeter patrols and eliminating the guard to their little prison. She knew that the events that actually happened were in no way that of him being a ninja, or some kind of highly trained operative. The man was unnaturally lucky, and made it all up as he went. The fact that by flying by the seat of his pants and he was still able to rescue not only her but nearly a dozen others was a miracle. She knew him as a hero, not just to her but to many in their group of survivors. He had saved many lives with his uncanny ability to get out of seemingly any jam, and she loved him dearly for it. She didn't love him just for saving her, of course. The man was an absolute gentleman, always willing to listen when she wanted to talk, even if it was for hours on end. Even in a zombapoc, he'd hold doors open for her, and make sure she got first bite from the MREs (Meals Ready to Eat). More than that though, there was a spark between them from the very beginning that grew into a raging fire by the time he had proposed to her. Somehow, he had found the time to find a ring that fit her, and would have cost a fortune pre-end times.

Now though, her face which had briefly been covered by a look of wonder was now etched with concern. Shepherd tossed and turned every night, his body becoming covered with sweat. Early on, she had woken him up to ask him if he was alright. Every time, he denied any knowledge of what was going on and she eventually stopped pressing him. Nights like this though, she lay awake and ran her fingers through his hair as he went through another fit of nightmares. She knew that he would never admit it, or maybe he just did not remember any of the dreams. The look on his face sometimes turned to that of pure agony as if he was reliving some horrible moment in his past, over and over again.

She knew though that nothing she could do or say could comfort him in his dream world. She had hoped, however, that just her mere presence, her hand on his cheek rubbing through his hair every so often let his subconscious know that she was indeed there and he was not alone. Shepherd had a mystery of a past, and that was something that everyone around him knew. He had never spoken of his past except, of course, his previous occupation which he got a kick out of telling others about. Many times, they called bullshit on him much to his pleasure. The stories that he told of his time rising up the ranks at a local grocery store from a bagger when he was fifteen years old to his position of a store manager before everything had fallen apart. Retail was hell, and he had weathered it with a positive outlook that no one could match. He had never once spoken about any family or friends, and had not allowed anyone, no matter how close to dig into his personal life. Someday, she'd figure it out though. *Someday*, Rachel thought to herself as she wiped what looked like a tear forming from his right eye. "I've got you," she whispered quietly into his ear and watched his body relax as if in direct relation to her comment.

"Forever and always."

Chapter One

I awoke with a start, my shirt clinging to my chest with sweat pouring from me as if I had been working out in a sauna. I turned my head and saw that the angel beside me was still fast asleep. *She was such a heavy sleeper*, I thought to myself as I stood up as quietly as possible. I performed my usual routine of stretching, then heading down the hall to the shared restroom. Since we had taken up residence at the base, we had to get used to sharing a communal bathroom among other things. It didn't take me much time to adapt to it though. Military life was tough, and it required some sacrifice, of that, there was no doubt. Sharing bathrooms was the least of my worries in life anymore. I was much more concerned with things like zombies. Yes, zombies, the living dead. I still have no idea what caused people to get sick and die and reanimate, but I'm also no scientist. When hordes of walking zombie began to consume the country, I and pretty much everyone at this base went into survival mode. If somehow you've been surviving in a bunker safe and sound and don't know about the walking blight, please send me a ticket to wherever you are so I can pretend this all is a dream. Or a nightmare, rather. As I stood at a urinal and let loose my torrent of built up liquid, the door swung open and I looked up to see Kenneth enter. "Damn dude, you look like shit," I told him with a grin tugging at my not quite awake yet lips. He just shrugged and waddled over to the stall next to mine. "The woman's going to kill me," he said as he began to take care of his own business. "She won't let me sleep," he continued with his narrative. Men have a code of not looking other men in the eye while we take pisses or shits. It's just against the ever present man code. So I stared straight, my eyes completely focused on the bare wall in front of me. The boring concrete with literally no character. "Is it that bad?" I asked in response. "I'm still young and in the best shape of my life and she still just destroys me," he said, shaking his head. I barely caught the movement from the corner of my eye. I, of course, did not look over at him. "But did you die?" I said with my grin widening as I officially finished up with a couple of shakes. If you don't get it, don't ask. "Can I come sleep in your bunk?" he asked, and actually turned his face to me. Thank the heavens and Jesus' moth balls that I had finished just a moment before, therefore avoiding the violation of man code. "It's sex dude. How hard can it be?" I shrugged as I stepped away from the stall. I heard another patter of feet as Jennifer came into the restroom and headed for her own bathroom stall. She slapped Ken hard on the ass, causing him to jump slightly. Thank God for urinals or the poor guy's aim would have caused major spillage. Granted, this was not at all what I was expecting when I woke up this morning, but the look that he had of his hand getting stuck in the cookie jar was absolutely hilarious and well worth it. He zipped up but stayed at the urinal waiting for her to finish. "Hurry back to bed babe," she said with a wink and she passed us by, finishing up in what must have been record time. Washing her hands and then heading back to her bunk within a few moments. He looked into my eyes and I into his. I burst out laughing. I mean a true, guttural, gut-busting laugh that shook me to my core. He just stared at me as I did my thing for a good five minutes with tears streaming down my face. "My bad man," I said as I finally was able to regain myself. I walked with him out of the restroom and headed back towards our bunk rooms. His room came first and I waved to him as he flipped me the bird before closing the door behind him. In a somewhat jovial mode, I returned to my own room. Rachel was still asleep, and beautiful as ever. I stared for a few moments at her face, with hair covering a good one half of her soft face. I knew that in a heartbeat, that soft face could become the face of absolute death coming to claim my soul, but in this moment, it was as if God himself wanted to share her beauty with me. Within a few quick seconds, the moment was passed. One and then both of her eyes opened, one of them still hidden behind a curtain of dark brown hair. "Hey babe," I said softly as I sat down next to her on the bunk. She simply closed her eyes in response and pulled the pillow over her head. I couldn't help but smile. This woman was absolutely adorable. I ran my hand through her hair a few times and felt her breathing return to her normal sleep patterns.

I stood back up slowly, trying to be as stealthy as possible. My inner Ninja was just bursting at the proverbial seams. I had almost completely dressed when the building that our bunk room was in was rocked hard by an explosion outside. The residential area for the newcomers like us was built inside of one of the large aircraft maintenance hangars. Engineers had created apartment like rooms out of wood, with steel reinforcements. As we were officially a couple, we got one of the rooms on the ground floor. Single survivors were on the floors above, with ladders needed to go between the floors. A pulley system was rigged so that the upper floors could transport larger items up without having to strap the item to their back and carry it up the ladder. The smell of machinery and oil was always prevalent in the building but it sure as shit beat being outside in a tent. Rachel was up in a flash, gathering her own clothes as if she was a dancer in a well-rehearsed dance movie scene. I naturally had fallen to the ground, with one pant leg still empty of the necessary leg, and I was desperately trying to stand up to finish getting dressed. By the time that I had righted myself, and slapped the buckle on my belt, she was already throwing on her BDU and gathering her gear. Just before she headed out the door, she tossed my own gear at me and said, "Get your ass out here." To which I diligently followed, finishing dressing as we quickly moved through the wooden halls. As we broke through the emergency door, a wave of heat smacked me head on. It was not the heat of the New Mexico day, but the heat of a burning fire. Embedded into the side of our building was what was left of one of the large drones used by the military folk here at Cannon AFB. The wreckage was still on fire, and people had setup a fire line to douse it while they awaited the base fire trucks. This was, however, not the place for Rachel and I to be just now. Our response positions to any kind of incident was along the ever present perimeter fence that surrounded the base. We were both parts of the rapid response team assigned to handling threats that were a danger to the overall base. Rifles were distributed, and all of our eyes focused on the perimeter. Sandbags had been set up to provide steady firing positions all along the fence. We stood, ready for action, the sound of sirens having arrived in the direction that we had come. The smoke of the fire turned from an active black to steady grey as the fire was put out. After 30 minutes of no action, an intercom page announced to stand down through loudspeakers set up strategically around the base. Later, we learned that the incident was caused by a malfunction in the software for the Predator UAV that had crashed into our sleeping quarters. Normally, this would not be such a big issue, but this was the fourth UAV that had been destroyed in nearly as any days. The Air Force crews had repeatedly done inspections on all aircraft before allowing them to fly every day, and the UAVs were preferred with their almost no cost fuel, and the small amount of noise in comparison to a large jet or helicopter taking off while people are sleeping. Yet like clockwork, each of the UAVs was sabotaged in some crazy way that only really smart people can understand. At this rate, we were going to run out of UAVs long before we could use them effectively. *Who knows, maybe that's how they want it?* I thought conspiratorially. Rachel just shook her head as she watched my facial expression show the apparently always present signs that I was thinking about some conspiracy. The narrowed eyebrows, my features showing consternation and a stare showing I was miles away at that moment. As a whistle sounded to alert us to return back to base and return the weapons, the expression on my face changed. It had turned to that of a young man in love, or so I hoped. For all I knew, I was drooling on myself. I rushed her and gave her an epic kiss, damn near knocking her to the ground. She giggled loudly and pushed me away. "Calm down there, soldier," she said with another laugh as I stood straight up and made like a British Castle Guard. She slapped my shoulder playfully as we resumed our walk back to the residential area.

The what had once been a semi-raging fire had been since extinguished. We stood along with everyone else and their moms it seemed, to get a glance at what had been beneath the flames. The wreckage of the drone was quite the topic for discussion and with good reason. Rachel saw my face yet again contort into my conspiracy facial expression. She eye balled me for a moment before deciding to speak. "What are you thinking, Shep?" she said as I slowly moved my eyes from the wreckage over to her face. "Huh?" I said, somewhat confused. I seriously had not heard a thing. She sighed audibly. "What's on your mind?" "Oh," I said, taking a moment to collect my thoughts. "Since we boarded the helicopters from Albuquerque, nearly every aircraft has had some kind of malfunction. Mine was shot down sure, but what about the one you were on? What about all of the ones that were damaged before the horde attack? Now the drones are having problems. I don't like it. I feel like someone's messing with our toys on purpose." She stared intently into my eyes and probably into my soul for a minute or so. She nodded then. "I can understand your logic, but do you really think someone would do that though? What's their end game?" I shrugged, "I have no idea. I'd think that everyone would want to pitch in and help save as many people as possible. Who knows? Maybe they want to keep us contained here. Or maybe someone doesn't want us to have tools that can be used against them," I said sighing audibly. I checked my watch and it was now about time to get ready to go to work now. "Are you up for a quick run around the base?" I asked her. "You bet your ass I am," she told me with a grin and shot ahead of me. "Damn it, woman, I was not ready!" I shouted to her beautiful backside as I chased after her and we began our daily exercise routine before reporting for duty and starting another work day in the dead land that was now New Mexico.

Chapter Two

"Alright ladies and gents," my commanding officer, Dail, entered the room. He was a career soldier, crisp and clean cut with nothing on his uniform out of place or not perfectly centered. He was a soldier in his mid-20s, just a tad younger than myself. Part of me was a bit irritated at being ordered around by someone younger than myself but I'm not ignorant enough to take real offense at it. If someone younger than me has knowledge and experience that I myself do not have, then I will digress. I had seen this young soldier rally his troops in the battle against the horde, and I knew he was the real deal. He had raised the ranks as a leader and with so low of a supply of fully trained experienced soldiers, he had been promoted insanely rapidly. "Our mission today is to recon the former basecamp of the so-called 'Exiles' just a ways up north. Due to the air folks having issues with their birds, we will be going via Humvee convoy. Two hummers along with one of our few Strykers will head out in thirty minutes. I want everyone locked and loaded, and ready for anything. Initial reports say those idiots are all but extinct, but we all know what they say about assumptions," he said, glancing down at a sheet of paper on the table in front of him. "What's that Serge?" one of the men in the room asked in question. Sergeant Dail looked up and saw a young kid, around 18 or 19 years old, with a grin plastered on his smug face. "It makes an ass out of you and me," he said in response. A chuckle came from the 12 or so other people in the room. "Now, I have seating assignments here on the board," Dail pointed to the white board behind him. "I know what someone is going to ask, and no, you cannot switch seats. I'm not here to baby you. I'm here to make you all work. So cut the shit and do your job," he said, looking the young kid directly in the eyes. "Make no mistake people, because of the drones being out of commission, this is our first foray into that area since the attack. We have no real idea what we'll come across. Stay safe, and stay alive. Dismissed," he said with finality as we all stood to once again gather our gear.

Once we were all equipped, we headed to the motor pool for the vehicles. I was assigned to driver duty of the second hummer from the front. Every time I sat in the driver seat of one of these, I thought back to my bright yellow hummer that I had acquired in Tijeras and had to abandon in the desert outside of Tucumcari. As anyone who have ridden in military vehicles could tell you, they were not nearly as comfortable as their civilian counterparts. The smart ass kid from earlier was my passenger. Riding shotgun as it were. *This would be tons of fun*, I thought to myself as I closed my door and set my rifle by my side. Kenneth, Jennifer and Rachel were all assigned to other vehicles. The ladies were in the Stryker and Kenneth was riding in the gunner seat of the first hummer ahead of my own. Each of our hummers were mounted with 5.56MM M249 SAWs while the Stryker had a 7.62 MM M240 machine gun mounted. We could deal out some serious damage in a hurry. The Stryker was an absolute beast. The eight-wheeled troop carrier was massive, and heavily armored in comparison to our trucks. If the shit were to hit the proverbial fan, we were told to fold in behind that bad boy and let it handle anything coming our way. I completely agreed with that plan should it need to be enacted. Unfortunately, the base had a whopping two of these and one was always kept in reserve. The other downside of this foray was that even though we had the up-armored variants of Humvees, plenty of shit could still take us out. That fact continued to stress me out as the memory of my Evac chopper being shot down over Albuquerque just a few weeks ago came to the forefront. We had found no trace of whoever had shot us down, but if they had the capabilities to shoot down a helicopter, a slow-moving convoy would not be much of a problem. I began the process of starting my Humvee and checked the gauges. The wait light darkened and I turned the switch to on, and the diesel engine came to life. The folks in the motor pool took damn good care of these vehicles, but I sure as shit was not going to get caught in the middle of nowhere having run out of fuel, so I checked that gauge twice, even tapping on it just to be safe. I double checked and sure enough, it was a full tank. I heard the Stryker start up ahead of me, and a chorus of engines from behind. I saw Kenneth poke his head out of the top of the Humvee in front of me and wave in my direction. I smiled and waved back. We began to move, rolling forward slowly, letting people walking ahead of us pass. A dozen people stood guard at and around the main gate leading out of the base. Since our last brawl with undead, they were taking no chances. I waved to the last set of guards as we rolled out of the gate and onto the streets outside of Clovis, New Mexico. Our destination was what had been a small camp outside of Tucumcari. There, a group known as the Exiles had captured civilians and soldiers alike, and had killed a great many people in cold blood. The air force had made short work of them while they had been in pursuit of yours truly while I was attempting to escape from a rescue of a small group of women remaining at the camp, including Rachel. No part of that rescue went according to plan but we didn't die so I'll chalk that up as mark in the win category. While we had not seen nor heard of any of those bastards causing any more trouble, the base brass was not fond of the idea of letting a threat regain strength. So here we were.

As we rolled down the long-abandoned streets heading west for US 268 which would eventually switch to US 209. Pre zombapoc, it would have been about an hour and a half. Now with our convoy and our need to move around wrecks, it would probably take around three hours. As the miles ticked by, the kid beside me started to get restless. I personally am more than happy to just enjoy the drive. "Hey man, do you think we'll see any action?" the kid asked me, slapping my arm to get my attention. I shot daggers at him with my eyes but he continued undeterred. "Man, I'm so ready to shoot some shit. Zombies, bad guys, hell, I'd shoot a damn sign if I had the chance. Base is so boring." I lost interest very quickly and just focused on the road. I could still hear him droning on about how he's the baddest badass that ever lived and if anyone messes with us, he's going to take them on single-handed and so on so forth. *Teenagers man, no wisdom*, I thought as I drove along. The dude was hyped up like he was an 8-year-old girl and we were driving to Disneyland to see her favorite princess. We passed a row of abandoned cars and I saw the Humvee ahead of me slam on its brakes. I had barely enough time to hit my own brakes and come to a stop just mere inches from the rear of the vehicle in front. A group of 8 infected was walking along the right side of the road. I mean literally, off to the side of the road, as if avoiding the pathway of vehicles. They were moving in the opposite direction of our base and they barely acknowledged that we were there at all. They just continued walking along, as if without an undead care in the world. "Let's shoot those fuckers!" The kid on my right moved to jump out of the vehicle. My arm shot out to grab his uniform sleeve. I missed. He was already out of the truck and shooting. The loud staccato of rifle fire just outside the passenger door was deafening. Within just a few moments, all of the infected were dead, riddled with far more bullets than necessary. The kid jumped back into the Humvee with a huge shit-eating grin on his smug face. I, however, was not at all amused. I punched the kid with a fist so strong that it seemed to start somewhere down near the Rio Grande and hit him full force. The giddy kid was immediately silenced and knocked unconscious. Our particular Humvee was filled with supplies, so we had no other passengers. I know for sure others saw his little shooting stunt. After another moment, the lead Humvee once again began to move. The rest of the road trip was spent in blissful peace and quiet as the idiot next to me continued to slumber for the duration.

We arrived shortly after to the town of Tucumcari, New Mexico. The town was the last major stopping point before hitting the Texas border. It was one of those, eat here, fuel up here, or else you're going to die between here and the next town type of places. I'm not knocking it, they had some great food. It just always felt like if you didn't eat and get gas there before heading to Texas, you would be totally fucked. Not Far East of the town was the Tucumcari Metro Park. Within eyeshot of that park sat the husks of several trucks and motorcycles that had pursued us on the path away from the camp. The RV bus thing that we had used to escape was still there, though much worse for wear. It had canted to one side and was in danger of tipping over. We slowly passed the wreckage. Flashbacks of that whole ordeal came to the forefront of my mind as we passed the carnage. Bodies still lay in the road in their final resting place. Within a few minutes, we were at the former Exiles basecamp. Several more RVs and assorted vehicles still sat in a circle around what had once been their communal fire pit. The remainder of tents were blown all around the area, one was even stuck in a tree quite a ways from the site, maybe a quarter of a mile away. We pulled into the camp and piled out of our respective vehicles. Kenneth walked over to me after disembarking and pointed at my sleeping beauty in the passenger seat. "What the hell happened to him?" he asked with a concerned look on his face. "He hit his face and fell asleep," I told him in a deadpan tone of voice. He processed it for a moment, then a smile crept from ear to ear. He fist-bumped me and laughed out loud. I couldn't help it. Laughter is infectious and especially his laughter. A short woman with long black hair named Jaylin had the most seniority as far as people on this mission so she took charge. Generally, my rule is to use everyone's last names as they tend to be easier to remember but her last name was super long and took a ton of practice to pronounce correctly, so I'll leave it at Jaylin. "Alright everyone, form up. Let's check out the camp for anything useful. Keep an eye out for any kind of intelligence." We did just that, splitting up into teams. Other than another can opener, we had no real luck in the first two tents, but that was fine because even can openers were in short supply at base. The remaining clothes were old, worn and kind of nasty and there weren't many if any weapons left behind. They had all been armed when they came after me so that made a lot of sense. We came to our first RV, an older model with paint fading across the side facing the sun. The door had a lock on the outside, which goes without saying; caught my interest. Although I just said it, so does it really go without saying? Someone in the group was smart enough to bring bolt cutters and we cut the lock. As soon as we opened the door, the stench of feces and body odor flooded out of the trailer like a biblical flood wave. I damn near tossed my lunch right then and there, and several others in our team did just that, depositing their leftovers in the sand around the RV. I took a step in and saw right away that it was not a normal recreational vehicle by any means. It had been gutted, and it looked like the inside of a prison cell. One toilet sat in the far end with no door or privacy, a sink was where the kitchen had been and that was about it. I did, however, have to address the elephant in the room so to speak. Dead center (no pun intended) in the RV was a withered man covered in shit. I don't mean covered in stuff, I mean covered in actual human shit. I literally blurted out, "It stinks in there" as I covered my face with my hand as if that would somehow fix the stench. The man lifted his head ever so slightly. I immediately called out of the RV, "Medic! We need a medic in here now!" I yelled as loud as I could. I entered the trailer, moving my feet carefully, trying to avoid the piles of crap every few steps. A chain was attached from one of the man's ankles to the chair that was drilled into the floor. His hands were bound together in handcuffs. I took the sight of the man in. His wrists were beginning to scab over from the cuts and abrasions of him having tried to remove them by force. He was malnourished and close to death by starvation. The sink in the kitchen was just close enough for him to use, but it most likely ran out of water before too long. A medic; Ashmore entered behind me. After gagging herself, but recovering like a champ, she set her medical bag down next to the man in what she had hoped was a clear spot and got to work.

Chapter Three

We were able to move the man into the back of the Stryker. One of our team members had doused him with water from a gallon jug, much to the relief of all of us. I'd love to say the stench of shit was washed away and the crisp, clean smell returned, but unfortunately, this was not the case. It dampened it for sure, but wet shit kind of still smells like dry shit. The man eventually was able to mumble about how refreshing that it was. He drank from a canteen greedily, and ate two MRE crackers. Once he was in the vehicle and on the bench, he fell asleep, stretched out like a jungle cat. The medic continued to administer to him, even in his sleep. Kenneth was beside the medic and had helped her dress the wounds as best she could. "Long time no see doc," he had told her while helping her clean him up. I was standing security outside of the troop transport as they conversed. "I'm glad to see that bullet didn't kill you," she said in response, grunting as she moved the man over to his side. "Thanks, I think?" he asked her, remembering when she had dressed his own wounds after he was shot by a distraught mother, what seemed like years ago. "You're welcome," she said as she moved the man's hands to one side, getting a better view of his back. "Next time, don't get shot," she said. As if that somehow fixed everything. As if he had planned on getting shot. He sighed and shrugged. Just under his breath, I heard him whisper, "Ms. grumpy over here." I, of course, chuckled in hearing that and she immediately turned around to me. "Is something funny?" she asked with fire in her eyes. I immediately held out my hands in a placating manner. "Nothing, I almost sneezed," I said, throwing whatever was on the top of my head. I'm not sure if it worked or not, but she turned back around. *Whew*, I thought to myself as I too turned back around. The last thing I needed was another woman pissed off at me. Once the man was secured in the transport, the whole group of us had a huddle. Nothing besides some tools and other assorted items were found. Personally, I was just glad none of those assholes were still around. I did not want to get into another gunfight if I could at all help it. As we began to plan our next move, the door to my Humvee opened and slammed closed loudly. "Oh shit," I sighed, and turned to look at the kid who was now rapidly approaching. A visible bruise was forming on the side of his face, and his right eye was starting to swell halfway closed. "You bastard!" he yelled as he came straight at me. "Relax man..." I started and he cut me off. "Fuck you asshole, you hit me!" Isabel was beside me and raised an eyebrow in my direction. Just as he came within hand-throwing range, Kenneth grabbed him by the front of his shirt. "Listen, jerk off. Those infected were not a threat to our team. You were." The kid looked taken aback for a moment. So Ken pressed on. "You endangered all of us by getting out of your vehicle. If they had turned and attacked you, we would all have been forced to engage and people could have died for your stupidity. He did you a favor by knocking your ass out," Kenneth said, still holding onto him tight. The kid's eyes immediately turned to me and were still fairly full of menace. Ken shook him, and his eyes came back around to him. "If you had gotten anyone killed for that reckless stunt, I would have just shot you then and there and be done with it. You're lucky a little fist kiss is all you got. Now are you ready to get to work or should we put you down for another nap?" he asked the kid. The wind in his sails was deflating in record time. "Fine," he said like the petulant child that he is. "What's your name kid?" Ken asked as he finally let him go. "Arturo." "Alright, Arturo. We were thinking about going into town and checking for more supplies. Are you in?" After glaring at me another moment, he nodded. "Of course, I'm in," he said. With that, the tension was cut, and the group reformed into our huddle.

Ten minutes later, we were back on the road. I waved to the RV we had escaped in one last time as we passed by it. Several minutes later, we were in Tucumcari proper. We headed to what looked like a series of warehouses. The fast food places would be absolutely horrid so we knew we had to look for storage buildings for supplies. Whether it was canned food or building supplies, we'd take damn near anything. That was the state of survival these days. Find whatever you can and use it however you can. We pulled into the parking lot of a large warehouse building that unfortunately did not let on what was inside at all. For all we know, it was store shelving inside. However, when you're on the brink of survival, it's fairly important to make absolutely sure. We exited the vehicles. Two of our group stayed with the man rescued from his RV prison cell. The rest of us stacked up on either side of the entrance to the warehouse. On the right side of the door was Isabel, Ashmore, the medic, Atencio, an intense female soldier who had previously helped defend Cannon AFB, two guys who I can't seem to ever remember their names and lastly, myself. On the other side of the entrance was Kenneth, Rachel, Jaylin; the woman whose last name was too long for me to pronounce, another woman named Susan next and lastly, Arturo. The kid looked like he was chomping at the bit to get inside. I'm not even sure what that analogy means, but he was whatever that was. With a one, two and three, we entered. Both teams spread out along the interior walls on either side. The warehouse was completely dark. Flashlights popped on from down the line. Our lights swept the rows of shelving that we could see. It looked like it was a distribution center of some kind. This was absolutely a total score for the home team, one which was sorely needed. We began to move forward, each of us taking an aisle and heading towards the back of the building. I stopped in my lane and heard a tapping noise that I couldn't place. I listened intently and even tilted my head to one side as if that would help, like a dog hearing a high-pitched whistle. I happened to glance up and movement caught my eye. Above us were a series of catwalks that ran parallel to the aisles. Something was moving above us, and the tapping noise was the sound of feet on metal. "Hey guys," I said rather loudly, hoping to get everyone's attention. As if synchronized, the things above us jumped down and into each one of our aisles. I watched it in seemingly slow motion as a person, it was definitely a person, leapt down and landed right on me. With teeth chomping and drool drooling, I struggled to get it off of me, after having my breath expelled out of me. A light bulb lit up in my head. *Infected!* Shot through my mind and I fought back with increased fervor. I hit it repeatedly with the butt stock of my rifle right in the face.

Even while fighting for my life, I noticed something strange. Blood. Wet blood was being spilt as I hit the hell out of its head. It wasn't coagulated like the zombies we were used to at all, a mix of dark black sludge. This blood even felt hot to the touch. On my next swing, the infected dodged my next attack. Again, it didn't just take it like a normal infected. It moved back just enough to avoid the weapon. I turned to my side, seeing my chance. The creature tumbled over, having lost its balance. I got my feet under me and I fired two rounds from my rifle into its chest and was about to shoot it in the head when it slumped over and lay still. "What the actual fuck," I said to myself as I stared at the infected in disbelief. Chest shots had never killed an infected before. It was always only headshots. *What was going on?* I asked myself in a daze. I heard multiple gunshots going off around me and sprinted to the end of the aisle and into the next one. Three infected were in that one aisle, eating one of the guys that I couldn't remember their names. I lifted my rifle and shot six times into their backs. They too slumped over and lay still. I moved onto the next isle. Rachel had taken care of her new friends with little issue and had moved to assist Kenneth whose rifle had jammed. He was holding two infected at bay by swinging his broken rifle like a baseball bat. I saw it connect with one of their faces, causing fresh blood and bits of teeth to be ejected from its mouth, which was gross. Rachel dispatched them quickly and I moved to the next one down and saw another infected trying desperately to sink its teeth into Susan. I pulled the creature off of her and it skittered behind me as I did so. I fired one shot into its head and it lay still, bleeding from its head wound. "Thank you," she stuttered out as I lifted her to her feet. "No problem," I said as I handed her her rifle from the ground. Eventually, we cleared the remaining aisles. I came up on Atencio who I kid you not, was beating the shit out of one of the dead infected repeatedly. We all gathered around as she just kept kicking the thing. I eventually pulled her away from it. She still tried, bless her little heart but after holding her still for a moment, she relaxed.

I looked around and saw that we had lost three of our group. "Three dead just like that," I said quietly. Rachel shook her head,

"No, Arturo was right here. He was fine." We all looked around as if he would just magically appear from beside us. "Damn it," I said, and we once again spread out, this time in teams of two. I spotted the idiot at the end of the building, about to walk into the office area of the warehouse. "Stay where you are!" I shouted at him as I began to run his direction. "I've got this!" he yelled back. "You'll see!" he said as he entered the doorway. "No!" I shouted. He stopped dead in his tracks and lowered his rifle. I saw him look back at me as he was bowled over by four infected. They were tearing him apart before he even hit the ground. I fired, hitting two of the attackers as my rounds drilled into them. The other two continued to take bites from the poor kid, seemingly oblivious to what was going on around them. More rounds flew past me as the rest of the group followed in my tracks. I kicked the head of the last infected so hard, I heard and physically saw the neck snap, and bones protruding from the skin. I slid to a stop next to the boy. He gurgled, with blood erupting from his mouth. "Relax, we've got you," I said quietly as his eyes met mine. He knew, just like I knew that he was a goner. Even without the bites, there was nothing we can do for the amount of damage he sustained. "Did we win?" he asked, spitting out blood as he spoke. "Yeah buddy. We won." He seemed to nod with satisfaction as his head lay back onto the concrete floor of the warehouse and his eyelids flickered. Blood ran out of the tear in his neck like a river, coating my hands as it slowed to a trickle. Within another moment, life left those eyes forever. "Damn it, kid," I said with remorse as I closed his eyes one last time. I stood, and fired one round into his head before he could turn into one of the undead. Isabel and Rachel had cleared the rest of the offices with their teams. I gently lifted the kid into my arms and headed back outside once I was waved forward with the signal that it was indeed secure. We gathered the other two dead men and placed them into the back of our rides, each one received the mandatory bullet to the brain, just in case. We would mark this place on our map for resource collection. We were done for today. We'd return to base and have the all too well-known memorial service for people from Cannon. At this rate, we were going to be extinct sooner rather than later with all of the human lives lost since the fall. This was unsustainable and unfortunately for us, two other major players knew that as well, and they were counting on that very fact.

Chapter Four

We drove through the gate back into Cannon AFB, and headed for the motor pool. We parked our rides in a very neat fashion and proceeded to disembark. Crews were already waiting for us to help move the injured man to the makeshift hospital, and to transport the dead to be buried. All of us were exhausted. The short time that we were out of the fence; a whole 5 hours or so, had resulted in three deaths, one starved prisoner freed and the realization that things are not what they seemed with our undead friends. As if on cue, the man in charge of our unit, Sergeant Dail approached and wanted an immediate debriefing. Those of us left standing proceeded back to our meeting area and sat down heavily in the old metal chairs. "Can someone please tell me how the hell we lost three people on a reconnaissance mission?" he said with a look of frustration on his chiseled face. We all just kind of sat there, as if a teacher was wanting to know who put a thumbtack on their seat, and everyone knew but no one wanted to say anything. I figured I'd start the shit show, so I stood and looked him square in the eyes. I recounted the events from our leaving the base, to Arturo's killing of the walking dead, to the infected ambush. His eyebrows raised visibly at the telling of that whole bunch of shenanigans. After I said my piece, I sat back down once again as if I had just spilled my entire life story. He too sat with a sigh and ran his fingers through his short brown hair. "Are you absolutely sure that they planned the ambush?" he asked me. I looked back up at him. "Yes, sir. It was too coordinated. They absolutely caught us off guard. I know for sure that had I not seen them above on the catwalks, I would have never seen them coming at all. I'd be there with Arturo waiting to leave this god forsaken place." The rest of the group murmured their agreement. "A god-damned zombie ambush. That's fucking great," he sighed again heavily, and took a moment to think his thoughts through. "Alright. Go get some grub, and head to bed. You all have had a long day. Report back tomorrow morning at 0900 hours." With that, we all stood, saluted and headed out of the room.

Rachel was right on my heels as I left the room. I didn't turn back to look at her. The feelings that were going on within me were intense and varied to say the least. After everything that had happened with the kid; the loss of life and almost losing my own, I was lost in the abyss that was my inner darkness. During this damn apocalypse, I had lost everything that I had spent a majority of my life to build. Even the twelve years of schooling, from kindergarten to graduating high school had been nearly a complete waste of time. I sure as shit didn't learn how to reload ammo in the 9th grade, or how to stitch up a wound in 11th. Very little of my education had mattered at all in the long run. My adult life I had spent working my way up the corporate ladder to become a grocery store manager. Again, for what? What part of making sure my store displays looked great, and getting on my hands and knees to clean the bathroom tiles before a corporate inspection helped prepare me for where I'm at now? I continued down my freefall into darkness until Rachel literally grabbed me and pushed me against a nearby wall. Since my mind was completely elsewhere, it totally caught me off guard. I let out a grunt as I hit the wall. She pointed her finger of doom into my face. "Listen mister, you are not allowed to push me away. I get that you're upset. I get it babe, I do because I am too. I am here for you and we will get through this together," she said with a tone of voice that I knew meant that it was not up for negotiation. I stared at her a moment, with the 'Uh oh' finger still pointed squarely at me and nodded. "You're right. I'm sorry," I said, my head sagging lower. The stress and the sadness of the day weighing on me even more heavily as I stood there. She put her hand around my chin and lifted my eyes to hers. "Don't say that you're sorry. Just hug me," she said as she wrapped her arms around me. The woman was a damn magician with how she could just get around any walls that I had up inside. Like the Trojan horse of the Greeks, she eventually always got in, but like in a nice way. What could I say to her in response? Any man worth his weight in salt would know to defer and hug the woman. We're stupid sometimes, but not dumb. If that makes any sense. So I did just that and I wrapped my own arms around her, kissing her forehead and receiving a mouthful of hair for my trouble. The smile on her face though was absolutely worth every hair gagging second of it. "Now, let's go get some food and go back to bed. It's your turn to go first," she said with a wink and she took my hand and led me towards the mess hall. Like the soon to be husband that I was, I dutifully followed.

At 2:35am, or something like that, I awoke from another series of horrific dreams. This time, Rachel was awake and staring right at me. I stared back at her, feeling like I should be worried. I knew then that it was time to talk as this woman would stare into my soul and would reach right in and pull whatever she wanted out of my mind or body by force if she felt it necessary. Once again, taking it all in and deferring to her, I stood and walked the short distance from the bunk to the opposite wall by the doorway. The sweat on my body created a light sheen in the little bit of light filtering in from around the door. I put my arm on the wooden wall and stood there with my head resting against it. I heard her stand and follow me. She once again embraced me, hugging me from behind. I was one of those people that was always warm to others. Both emotionally and physically. In this case, I'm referring to physically which I attested it to being hot-blooded, but I know that's not really the case. On the plus side, it made me one of those people that everyone wanted to cuddle with, simply because I was warm as hell to the touch. "Talk to me," she whispered into my ear. I sighed, both outwardly and inwardly. It was going to happen sooner or later and one way or another. I turned around and saw her gorgeous eyes staring back into mine. "Alright," I said as I led her back to the bunk and sat down. She sat across from me with crossed legs. I, for one, do not know how adults can still do that. Every time that I had ever attempted crisscross applesauce, it hurt the hell out of my legs. She just stared at me as my thoughts traced back around to the present. "Alright," I said quietly. "You said that already," she told me with no small amount of expectancy. I sighed out loud again and began to speak. "You know about my previous career." She nodded and moved her hand in a 'continue' gesture. "I was married with a baby on the way before the world ended." She looked at me completely stunned. "What?" she whispered as she looked into my eyes, tears already beginning to form. I nodded and began to tell her my story, with tears of my own not far behind.

"When the zombapoc began, I was the store manager of a local grocery store in the heights. The heights in Albuquerque were regarded as the high-end neighborhoods. The well off, the high class, whatever you wanted to call them lived in and around the northeast heights. Before becoming a store manager, I had worked my way up from a bagger to a cashier to pretty much any position that I hadn't previously worked before. I was the jack of all trades type of person. I had met this wonderful girl when I had first started and I fancied her something fierce right away. She was one of those chicks that everyone found attractive and she did not have a hard time getting attention. I'm not sure when it was that I went from just one of those other guys working at the store to the one who caught her eye. To be honest, I don't even know when I made the leap from the bagger who was so socially awkward that I couldn't look customers in the eye when I asked them how they were doing that day, to full-blown won't shut the hell up type of person. I was always truly a shy kid, the kind that played video games, ate Doritos and drank mountain dew almost exclusively. When I made the leap into her line of sight though, my entire world changed. When she gave me her attention though, I changed almost overnight. I started to become the man that I knew I could be. It took a shit ton of work. For the first time in my life, I spent money on clothes, I got a stylish haircut and so on. It was really the first time in my life that I felt powerful. When we began to date, it was the most amazing thing that I had ever experienced. Fast forward a few years later, and several more promotions later, she was still the facet of my fascination. Gorgeous, free-spirited and someone that I wanted to spend forever with. Things began to get rocky shortly before the apocalypse. Being in such a position of responsibility and working so many hours caused me to neglect the things that really mattered in life. The new Xbox games that had just been released and my now wife. That was a joke by the way. My wife was the most important thing in my life and everyone around me knew it. She told me shorty after my taking the store manager position that she was pregnant. I was naturally on cloud nine. I was both freaking out and thrilled to bring a new life into the world, a new little Shepherd. However, as the work hours continued to rise and my attention continued to leave her, things got bad. I won't go into details about our marital issues as it's fairly mute at this point. My hobby had quickly turned from playing co-op on Left 4 Dead to purchasing a pistol and going to the range over and over again. That was my getaway from the world. I suppose in the end, it paid off. In fact, after the end of the world had come, I had an opportunity to regain some of my pride by shooting a certain guy in the head. Don't worry, the guy was dead, or undead rather. It was an absolute pleasure to move him from undead to dead dead. It was the loss of not only my wife but the child that had put me at the edge of suicide. As the world was burning around me, I sat in an empty home. One that had once been filled with laughter, with moans of pleasure and with the occasion sounds of a horror flick or Netflix series. With the sirens in the background, and the screams outside, I sat in the dark with a pistol to my head and a bullet in the chamber just chomping at the bit to be released from this life's confines. I never did pull the trigger though. It would have been too easy. I deserved all of the pain that I felt, or so I thought. As the hordes of refugees left Albuquerque, I stayed put. I didn't have the energy to leave with those hundreds of people. I would live or die at home, slowly but surely going through my remaining liquor supply. It was not until a fire started in the housing complex that the decision was made for me. In emotional pain or not, the idea of burning alive was scary as shit. I left the home with my pistol, two magazines of ammunition, an extra box in my pocket and a backpack filled with what little survival gear I had stashed away.

I ended up walking for two miles before I came across two people running from a pack of zombies. I watched them with morbid fascination as the infected followed their every move. It wasn't until one of them tripped and fell that I stopped my onward progress. The two people were obviously a couple, as before the trip to the ground, the man had been pulling the woman's hand behind him, pulling her forward. I heard an audible snap as one of the woman's bones broke with the fall. My guess was it was her foot, as it looked like it got snagged on an open storm drain. The man was trying to protect her, and was thus far holding his own with what appeared to be an old wooden baseball bat. It was not until another group of infected, numbering eight, appeared and joined their brethren that he began to lose steam. Something inside of me, maybe empathy, or memories of being a chivalrous gentleman, to this day, I'm still not sure what it was. Something flicked a switch inside of me and I went from casual observer to rescuer. I pulled my pistol, a Ruger 9mm and fired round after round into the heads of the zombies. In no time flat, I had the group of undead fuckers eliminated. The man, was now standing between me and the woman, as if guarding her from me. I just stared at him. "We don't want any trouble," he said with his weapon of choice. I saw more movement down the street heading our way. "You should help her get up and go before more of them get here," I told him as I stood between the duo and the incoming groupies. "You can't take them on your own," he said as he stood beside me. I grabbed his shoulder and turned him to me. "Take her and go. Find a safe place. Take care of her. Nothing is more important than that right now," I told him, looking into the teenager's eyes. He stood staring back into my own eyes and eventually nodded in agreement. He walked back to the woman, and helped lift her up. She let out a loud yelp as she stood, trying desperately to not place any weight on her right foot. He supported her weight, with her arm around his shoulder. He looked back at me as if to ask for permission. "Go kid. I've got this. Good luck," I told him as I turned back to the incoming group of infected. With that, they left. I truly hoped that they would make it. I never did see either of them again.

As I squared off with the new group, something caught my attention, or someone rather. A beautiful woman was about half way in the group of infected. The group was mid-sized with over a dozen or so. The woman though, kept grabbing my attention. Even from a distance, she looked familiar. When I realized just who she was, I hit my knees right then and there in the roadway. The woman, with an extended belly was my wife. My pregnant wife that had previously left me was there on the street, heading my direction, infected. The thought of joining my love passed through my mind. Maybe we would be happy together in death. It was not until the pain and the anger of the betrayal carved its way back into my mind that I slowly picked myself up off of the asphalt. I lifted my pistol once again and I fired the remaining rounds of ammunition left in my magazines, save for one final round. I stared at her as she shambled towards me. The formerly pregnant love of my life made it within a foot of me and I did not see a single spark of recognition or intelligence. She didn't know me, and I would no longer know her. She was not the woman that I fell in love with anymore. With that dawning of realization, I raised my pistol and fired the last round point blank into her head. I caught her as she fell, and I gently laid her down onto the road way, chivalrous to a fault. As I stood back up, I took one last look at her, and down at the baby bulge that she had been carrying for five months. I put my hand gently on the belly, hoping to maybe feel something. A kick maybe. Her skin was almost ice cold to the touch, and I felt nothing else. No signs of life from my would-have-been child. I left my hopes and dreams behind with them as I turned and walked away from my past and into the sunset, or whichever cliché works best."

I snapped out of my memory and saw Rachel beside me visibly crying. Looking around slowly, I realized that I was not on that street in the thick of it and I too officially broke down. I cried into her arms, and her into mine. I don't think I had ever cried as much as I did that night, but I'll be damned if it didn't help.

Chapter Five

Many miles away in the New Mexico desert, a series of TV monitors were hung along the wall of a posh office space. Directly across from the screens sat a brown mahogany desk. Adorning the desk was a series of photographs of various people in fancy gold lined picture frames, a very expensive clock and a nameplate with gold trim. 'Praetor Julius Hart' it read. Behind the desk, sitting in an extremely expensive leather office chair was a short, unhappy looking grey-haired man. The man was fairly plump as far as people in the zombie apocalypse were. It was apparent that while people were fighting over a can of spam, this man was not only well fed, but would send food back if it wasn't made exactly how he liked it. The man was on his office phone, and swung his chair back and forth as he listened to the voice on the other end of the line. "Yes dear," he said into the phone in a tired voice. "Okay. I'll see you at dinner. Love you," he said as he hung up the phone. He sighed. He honestly could not stand his wife and only brought her here when the shit went down to continue his uninterrupted claim to power. He would look weak if he had let his wife become one of those things. Now that she was here with him in the bunker though, it made him slightly regret it. His secretary, a gorgeous blonde who always wore a tight-fitting black dress knocked on his door. "Enter," he said. She did just that, closing the door behind her and walked over to him. She looked around the room to make sure no one else was there and proceeded to sit on his lap. The old man smiled broadly as the twenty-something bombshell stirred his loins. "You have a meeting in an hour with the General, and another meeting with the council in three hours," she said with a wink and she ground into his lap. "Thanks, dear," he said to her, grinning ear to ear. She stood back up, and he gave her a light slap on the ass. She giggled as she walked from the office and back to her desk just outside of the door. He was sure that his wife knew that he was having an affair, but even he knew his wife wasn't stupid enough to tell anyone about it. It would not end well for her at the very least, and he had had people killed for less. As she left, he continued to marvel at her backside until she was out of the room. The door closed with a well-oiled light click. His smile faded as he glanced back at the monitors on the wall. One of the monitors had a full live satellite image of Cannon AFB. The group that he had helped found called themselves the 'New World Order'. Not to be confused with the Japanese dance troupe of the same name, of course. The group consisted of men and women from the House of Representatives, the Senate, and even a select few from the White House and Pentagon. Established decades ago with the hope of world domination, many of those selected had different views on what the new world should be like, and many more views of why it had to change. Some felt the poor had to be purged. Others felt that if they reboot the world, they would no longer have to fear the elections and remain in power. Some even deep down wanted the extreme, a place to rule where they could do anything that they wanted with no fear of repercussion. Human nature with the veneer of our current society removed could be a truly cruel thing. There will always be do-gooders, of that everyone was sure of. Some felt that those individuals be convinced to stand down by words, bribery or just torture and be forced to join the winning side. Others, like Julius, knew better. Do-gooders like the ones at Cannon AFB needed to be wiped from the face of the Earth if they were to have the best chance at restarting this post-apocalyptic world into what it should be. A world ruled by the powerful, with one military that also policed its own citizens. Of course, with capital punishment for any that do not fall in line, and rewards for those in power. Just imagining such an Eden always brought his mood up. Julius though could not seem to get Cannon out of his mind. The fact that they had been unable to vacate the occupants did not sit well with him at all. He sat and stewed as he stared at the monitor that was the single focus of all of his efforts as of late.

Before he had realized it, the hour had passed. A strong knock came to the door and snapped Julius from his thoughts. He adjusted his seat and spoke. "Enter," he said briskly. The man in full dress uniform, General Hawkings entered stiffly. He stood in front of the desk at attention. The man, recently promoted had been called to the office to create a new plan to remove those being housed at Cannon so that they could capture the needed equipment from the base. His promotion had been due to his previous General being retired from duty via a 9mm bullet to the head. They had no room for failures in this new world. "Reporting as ordered sir," General Hawkings stated, once again snapping Julius out of his thoughts. "Yes, I can see that," he responded to the military man in front of him. He did not ask the General to sit, because he had not earned it yet. "What are you going to do about those people in my base?" Julius said to Hawkings. "My staff and I are forming several plans as we speak sir." "Such as?" he asked, his annoyance starting to grow. "Sir, we are looking at contaminating their water source, doing a HALO drop with some of our Special Forces, utilizing nerve gas or biological weaponry." The General focused on the imaginary spot above the head of the Praetor. "Good. Good," Julius said, his annoyance waning. "When you have a plan finalized, come speak to me so we can appropriate the required tools and manpower," he told the General. He nodded, and turned to walk out of the room. "Oh and Hawkings?" The General stopped and turned to look at the man behind the desk. "I'd suggest you don't fail us like your predecessor. You're an up and coming star in our new world, I'd hate to lose you." Hawkings for a moment lowered his gaze to the big man's eyes, before snapping them back up. "Understood sir," he said before turning back and leaving the room, once again, the door closed with a soft click.

Chapter Six

Kenneth was exhausted to say the least. Between their near-death experience at the hands of the zombie ambush, and the absolutely insatiable sexual demands of the woman in his bed, tired was two weeks ago. He needed a break, of that he was sure. As he sat up in the bed, trying his damndest to not wake up the sleeping nymph next to him, he realized that he had been so busy as of late that he had never really unpacked from Lucaya. Lucaya had been their apartment complex home before arriving at Cannon AFB and had been overrun in one last attempt to hold the line. They had lost several good people including their leader, George. The memory of that old man made his heart skip a beat. He then thought about the backpack that had been with him since the beginning. The old beaten backpack that at one time was used for school. He had tried the college route, going to CNM, a local community college. He realized real damn quick that school just wasn't for him. Kenneth was a free soul and wanted to make his own way. After spending hundreds on books that went unused, supplies and even that brand spanking new backpack, he dropped the courses. He began streaming his video game conquests live and while he was no celebrity, it helped him make a living. He hadn't needed much, enough for new games, to pay the bills and $50 a week for food and gas and he was set. He honestly had not even dealt much with dating, and had no real luck at it. The fact that now he had this woman, Jennifer, attached at his hip was quite a surprise for him. He slid out of the bunk, dedicating every fiber of his being to not waking the beauty before him. Somehow, he managed to sneak out of the bed. In the small adjourned closet, buried under military gear and a pile of women's shoes. That made him stop in his tracks for just a moment. *How the hell did she get so many shoes in this kind of situation?* He thought to himself. He moved the pile of shoes aside and found what he was looking for. A forgotten abused dark blue backpack. One of the pockets had been ripped from the pack, one of those times an infected got too close. He slowly unzipped the pack and began to pull items out. As he pulled items out of the pack, he evaluated each item. A small batch of some old clothing in need of a good wash, to which he almost fell backwards after taking a sniff. He tossed them to the side. Next, he found a small photo album. He had forgotten all about it. In his haste to vacate his apartment, he had grabbed only a few items. The album had an assortment of pictures dating back since his childhood. Photos of the brown-haired boy playing in the rain, on a camping trip with his parents and even him in one of those striped shirts that no kid would be caught wearing these days. His growing up had been rather painful. As a gamer to his core, his father had turned him onto games all the way back when the first DOOM game was released. Since those days, he was hooked. It royally pissed off his father when his young son began to kick his ass every match. Oddly, they stopped playing together after that. The photo of him holding a game controller at the age of 6 brought a smile to his face. As he flicked through the pages, he passed the full pages and entered the empty ones. His smile slowly vacated his face as he flipped through the empties. Would he even be able to take more photos to put into this book? Would they even be able to print photos in a year from now? The thoughts he was having was depressing to say the least. He gently placed the photo book to the side and put his hand in the pack, feeling for the next item. He pulled out a charging cord and plug. He for the life of him could not remember why he had this in his pack. Somewhat mystified, he set the items to the side. At the bottom of the pack was an MRE, Meal ready to eat or meals rarely edible depending on your relationship with them and a dead cell phone. The phone in his hand was something that he never thought he'd see again. The devices these days were fairly useless with the only real modes of communication being radio or satellite phones. He flipped the phone around in his hand. The old IPhone had seen better days. The case was rather beat up and thankfully, he had purchased one of those near destructible cases. The thought then occurred to him that he had the charger for it. The base had power. He might actually be able to salvage some of the more recent photos in his phone and be able to print them out while they still have a ready supply of ink on base. "What in the world are you doing?" Isabel asked him quietly as she turned over to look at him. "I forgot that I had this," he said, lifting it up to show her. She raised an eyebrow. "Does it work?" she asked. He shook his head. "It needs to be charged, but they didn't exactly install outlets in all of our rooms," he said, looking around the room. "Come back to bed, and in the morning, we'll get it charged and go from there. Deal?" she asked him. He nodded, placing the phone and charger onto the top of his pack and walking back to the bed. "I hope there's nothing important on it," he said as his head once again hit the pillow. "I'm sure it can wait," she said, closing her eyes and drifting back off to sleep.

Chapter Seven

I awoke slowly, stretching my arms out and accidentally punching Rachel softly in the face as I did so. She took it like a champ though and just rolled over. I realized what I had done, still half asleep and whispered an immediate "I'm sorry." She responded by very quickly and eloquently shoving my ass off of the bed. I landed with a thump and a loud 'Ooof.' I decided to take a moment while I was on ground level to continue to stretch. I then looked up just in time to see an avalanche of pillows and a blanket come crashing down onto my face. I slowly removed the said items from my face and saw that Rachel was already up, heading for the restroom. "Awesome," I mumbled as I proceed to pick myself up and follow behind her quickly. That amazing backside, even with her pajama pants was still an attention grabber. Any guy knows that it doesn't matter what their significant other wears, they will always look damn fine in it. In this case, she was wearing an old pair of sweats and a worn-out Green Day t-shirt. I damn near ran over a small child who was also heading to the restrooms as I stared longingly at that wonderful butt. "Oh shit, I'm sorry," I told the little boy that I had nearly sent sprawling on the floor. He regained his composure, and gave me an evil look. "Yeah, no problem," he said as he stared at me like I just asked him if he'd sell his soul to the devil for Cheetos. I use the term little boy loosely as he was maybe 10 years old. "A little piece of advice," I told him as I moved to get by him. "Don't get between a man and his lady," I said with a grin. The kid literally stood back in front of me, cutting me off. "Like this?" he said with a grin as he did so. I came to a halt. "Yeah, like that, don't be a douche," I told him as my own grin turned to frustration. "You're one of the soldiers, right?" he asked me. I looked the kid up and down. "Sort of. Why?" I asked slowly. "My friends are still out there," he said. "What's your name?" I asked him as I'm sure my face showed more than a hint of suspicion. “Matthew,” was his one-word reply. “Okay, Matthew. Who are your friends?” I knew full well that we had just recently been in the middle of a series of skirmishes with a band that had gone by the name of the Exiles. The last thing that I wanted was a kid who wanted to take me out for any of them being killed or left to fend for themselves. “Cara and Cayden and Joe and Raul,” he said quickly. “Are they kids?” I asked. He nodded in reply. I let out a breath and stood up straighter. “I’m sure if you let some of the people in charge know, they might be able to find them. If they’re still alive, they’ll find them,” I said, making a move to get past the kid. I suddenly had to urinate like it was no one’s business. He again stopped me. I then noticed Rachel watching us from the door to the restrooms, her curiosity apparently peaked. “I did tell them. No one even cares. They’re out there and they need help,” he said, an obvious look of frustration and anger flashing on his young face. “What do you mean by no one even cares?” I asked him, looking him straight in the eyes. “I told every adult that I could find. They either don’t believe me or just say, ‘we’ll take care of it’. But they don’t actually care. No one has even asked where they are," he said. I saw Rachel's eyebrow rise, and I knew this had to get settled before she came and intervened. I am a man after all and I wanted to sort this out like a man without her getting involved. "Why didn't your friends come with you when you came here?" I asked. "I was out looking for more blankets and this couple found me. They made me come with them and wouldn't look for my friends. I didn't even get to say goodbye," he said. "Alright, Matthew. Tell me where they are." He did just that, giving me directions and letting me know about their apparent hideout. I know my face which was rapidly growing into a look of dismay. Albuquerque. The kids were in Albuquerque. It was there that I had lost my whole world, and where the helicopter that I had been riding was shot down. Not to mention the lion that attacked me, the horde that chased us along Route 66 and in the end, losing my companion, Rodriguez, with whom I had grown very close. "They found a place to hide," he continued, my attention having waned to the past. I refocused and listened closely. "Alright, where is that place?" I asked a bit apprehensively. "Monte Vista Elementary

School," he said matter of factly. "Shit," I sighed, standing back up. That school was almost dead center in the middle of Albuquerque. I looked at Rachel who was now staring directly back at me. "Alright kid. Let me see what I can do," I told him as I stared into Rachel's eyes. The child kicked me in the shin, causing me to let out a yelp. "That's not good enough!" he shouted at me as my eyes came down to his. "Alright, Alright!" I said back as I saw him ready for round two. "I'll get them, alright?" I said, my hands out in a now placating manner. My shin was throbbing but the kid visibly relaxed. Rachel nodded and walked over to me. "Hey Matt," she said sweetly, wrapping an arm around him. "How about we go back to your room and we let him go pee," she had a grin as she led him away. I realized that I did indeed still need to go, like right then, and bolted for the restroom. After the piss to end all pisses, I stood in the stall with my hand against the wall. The kid's friends needed help. Who I am to say no? Although what if they were already dead? Would it be worth the risk of my life to try to find out? I literally held out my hands as if weighing my options. Should I just tell him that we looked but didn't find anything? That would make me feel like a total ass bag. Undecided, I headed back to my room still in a bit of a daze. I walked in, shutting the door behind me. Rachel was standing in the middle of the room, staring at me. "We're going," she said simply. I stood there, sort of puzzled. As my mind finally caught up to what she was talking about, I began by saying, "But..." She brought up her finger of doom. "We're going to make sure. We will be fine. We've been there before and if there is an off chance there are some children who need our help, we're helping them," she said, leaving no room for argument. As a man, I felt I had to bring my foot down hard on this one. So I said, "Okay dear" and that was that.

"So, what's this about road trip?" Ken asked me at breakfast. Isabel, Ashmore, the medic and Atencio were at the table as well and perked up at the question. Jaylin, one of the women rescued from the Exiles camp was behind me at another table and she too turned around. "Ummmmm what?" I asked slowly, the food in my mouth making it sound much more like an 'mmmmmm waf?'

Everyone, including Rachel was staring at me. She at least shook her head slowly in what could have been disappointment. I chewed and swallowed quickly, conscious of everyone watching me. I finished the last bit quickly and sighed, taking a drink of water from a plastic cup on the table. "Are you serious right now?" Atencio asked, her tone not at all cheerful. "Sorry, I was thirsty," I said defensively. "You've had your drink, now spill it." I tipped over what little water remained in the cup and gave her a wicked grin. She stood up, and made to come at me so I laughed and put my hands out, "Okay, Okay." She slowly sat back down. I recounted to the group about everything that had happened with Matt. I naturally left out the ass chasing. As much as I had no problem at all with describing that, I knew Rachel would choke me out in no time if I went off in that direction. As I finished up my tale, it was silent among the group. Jaylin had changed tables, tired of staying turned around, and sat with us. "So when are we leaving?" Ashmore asked. "I'm sorry, what?" I asked her, genuinely confused. "What?" she asked back, compounding my confusion even further. "She wants to know when we are all leaving," Atencio asked me. "Well, Rachel and I were going to leave tomorrow…" "What about me?" Ken asked from beside me. He seemed confused and maybe a bit upset at not having been included. "I can't speak for you man, I just figured we could do this ourselves," I told him. He moved his mouth to my ear, "I have got to go dude. She's going to drain my life out if I stay here with her," he said, a hint of fear in his voice. "Fine," I said, another one of my stupid grins starting to form on my face. "And us, of course," Atencio said, pointing to Ashmore and then herself. I raised my hand to protest as Isabel and even Jaylin piped up and volunteered. "I appreciate the help, really, but it's not your fight," I said, trying to calm everyone down. "You're going to need a medic if those kids need help," Ashmore said. I nodded, "Okay yeah, true…" "And you'll need another soldier to protect the medic," Atencio said. "I guess, but…" "And you'll need more soldiers to help protect the kids. I think two more ought to be enough," she continued, cutting me off and pointing to Jaylin and Isabel. I just shut my mouth, as there was no point. Thoroughly defeated, I sighed and spoke. "Alright fine, but it's on you. Don't blame me if you get hurt," I said. With that, we began to formulate a plan for leaving the next day. We would take two Humvees, and make sure that we were fully armed and well supplied. This would not be a repeat of my escape from Abq. We would be prepared for anything, or so I hoped.

Chapter Eight

We packed what little possessions that we had. Sargent Dail had graciously allowed us to fill up on ammunition for all of our weapons. He also let us requisition two Humvees for the occasion. I'm sure that it had more to do with having more vehicles than they needed and less to do with his feeling that the mission would be anything more than a complete failure. Frankly, I didn't care as long as we got what we needed. He wasn't willing to part with the gun-mounted Humvees, but the unarmed ones would be fine for this outing. Ashmore, Atencio and Jaylin all showed up and began stowing equipment. "Hi," I said, waving. They threw bag after bag into the vehicle. "You're taking all of that?" I asked, a bit bewildered at the sheer amount of stuff filling the truck. "Yes, don't be a dumbass," Ashmore said as she too threw her three pack into the first Humvee. "Wow thanks," I told her as I felt a mix of emotions range through my body, the mix ended with sarcasm. Rachel chimed in with a less than enthusiastic "yay." That, of course, caused me to grin. It was then that I realized that I'd be in the lead Humvee with not one but three women. Three of which could turn hostile at any moment. Any man that has ever been in this type of situation knows exactly what I'm talking about. Where any wrong move, wrong breath even could spark a complete riot. I was going to tread as lightly as possible for this whole damn adventure. In the next Humvee were Jaylin, Isabel and Ken. I saw him grimace as he saw the women all pile into my vehicle. With pleading eyes, I waved to him and got into my driver seat. I sighed quietly, as I knew I was about to embark on a long ass ride. Rachel 'accidentally' nudged me with her elbow while moving a bag around. "Oh, I'm sorry," she said oh so sweetly. I knew better though. I was already failing at my attempt to avoid the wrath of the ladies in the vehicle. We slowly pulled out of the gate and headed west, in the direction of Albuquerque, New Mexico. We were going to attempt to make it there with all haste and check on the kiddos. If they were surviving, we were going to relocate them back to Cannon AFB. Albuquerque had once been a growing city of a little over half of a million residents. With a growing nightlife, a huge variety of new craft breweries and restaurants, it was becoming a great place to live. Since the fall though, it was sitting in ruins just like every other city pretty much anywhere in the world. We followed US Route 60, heading away from the base. It would be about 55 miles until the first turn which would lead us through Fort Sumner, New Mexico. From there, we would take US-84 and then turn into Interstate 40. From there, it should be relatively smooth sailing back to Albuquerque, or so I hoped. For most of the trip, it was easy going. We saw the sights, and the smells of the glorious countryside. We had the good graces of having all of our windows down when we passed by what had once been a cattle farm that stretched for what seemed like forever. Have you ever had an odor just invade your vehicle all of a sudden, and no matter what you did to get rid of it, it stayed in your car for what seemed like an eternity? That was this kind of smell. Rotting half eaten cattle lay sprawled out as far as we could see on one side of the road. Even with the windows rolled up, we still continued to die a little bit inside as we finally pulled away from the farm. After driving several miles away, I pulled over, letting everyone get some fresh air. We rolled down the windows so that we could air out the vehicles as well.

"That was fun!" Ken yelled to me from his Humvee. I looked back and saw him sticking his head out the driver side window. I couldn't help but laugh, the picture of a dog driving with its head out of the window popped into my head. He naturally didn't get the joke so he pulled his head back in. Once everyone was piled back into the vehicles, we began to move again. It wasn't long before we came upon the signs for Fort Sumner. The mostly rural area began to give way to the occasional commercial building. A tractor company here, a tire shop there. The first big business that we came upon was the Motel 8. "What I wouldn't give to sleep in one of those rooms," Atencio whispered, I think to herself, but it was loud enough for us all to hear it. As we came up to the actual building, however, we could see that it was gutted. Half of the building was burnt down. The remaining half was open and exposed to the elements. "I doubt that they'd have acceptable accommodations right now. You're welcome to try though. Maybe they'll give you a discount," I told her quietly. A small chuckle arose from the other occupants of the car. The hotel had had a full parking lot of cars. All of which would probably never be driven again. One of the cars stuck out, what had once been a beautiful fire engine red Tesla was parked in the group. A forgotten longing came over me as I watched that one car as we passed by. It had been my dream car, to own one of those. The full package, of course, the ability to have it drive autonomously. *Those were the days,* I thought as it disappeared from the rearview mirror. The Billy the Kid museum passed by shortly after. Odds are the relics would be there forever, never to be uncovered. As long as that building too didn't burn anyway. Future generations, assuming that we survived long enough to procreate enough to have future generations, could visit that place, hopefully. Another thought crossed my mind at just how much world history had been lost in just the past few months. The countless other museums, art galleries, libraries that no doubt had been destroyed by nature or by arson. I shook my head quickly to dispel those thoughts. I couldn't allow myself to fall down that hole of despair, thinking about the past and what we've lost. We have to focus instead on what we're going to build, the books that we're going to write, the music and the architecture that will be this new generation's heritage. My thoughts had completely filled up my mind and it wasn't until I heard Rachel yelling in my ear that I snapped out of it. Ahead, a pile up of cars lay directly in our path and we were barreling towards them at high speed. Which is relative for those that have actually been in a Humvee and know they are by no means sports cars. Still, I stepped on the brakes, feeling someone smash into the back of my seat as I did so. Smoke erupted from our tires as they squealed, attempting to come to a halt. Kenneth had a much quicker reaction time and was slowing much more efficiently than I was. We tenderly kissed the leading car with our bumper and came to a stop. I turned to the women who were all disheveled in one way or another. All eyes slowly met mine and I saw what could only be described as a life-ending explosion of fiery anger coming my way. I did the only manly thing available to me and vacated the vehicle as quickly as physically possible.

I surveyed the mess in front of us. Cars, trucks, semis were tangled up in each other for at least a block. "This is nice," I said out loud as I looked over the vehicles. I heard the doors behind me open and close as the other occupants got out and were also looking at the pile up. I heard some light chatter from behind me and then footsteps as someone walked up behind me. "Whoa," I heard from my right. I glanced over, Ashmore was there. "What?" I asked her. She pointed towards the middle of the group of cars. "I thought I saw something move," she said, staring intently at the spot that her finger was now guiding my eyes to. As we both stared, I did see something, but only for a split second. As I looked on, something else moved three cars away and just inside the corner of my peripheral, I saw what looked like the top of a bald head pop up for just a moment then dip back down. "Uh oh," I said quietly, slowly backing up towards our vehicle. I think Ashmore caught sight of something as well, as she too was stepping back. "Hey guys…" she said, trying to get the other attendees' attention. I grabbed my rifle, and pulled it up to my shoulder. I had just enough time to raise it when the first of a terribly fast infected bounded over the lead car and headed straight for me. I flicked the safety to semi-automatic and fired two rounds, one into its chest and one into its head. The bullets caused the body's trajectory to change midflight, sending it just to the left of me. The now lifeless body landed onto the hood of my Humvee. I heard other rounds going off around me as the cars became alive with infected, like a previously hidden wasps' nest. These infected were unusually fast, running back and forth and climbing over cars in their way to get to us. They were doing a remarkable job of avoiding our projectiles, swerving back and forth every few steps. Don't let anyone ever tell you that hitting a moving target is easy. It's not. I saw Ashmore go down to my right, an infected grasping for her. Atencio wound up a kick and with the steel toe of her boot, kicked it directly in the head, sending it flying backwards with an impressive indent in its face where its nose used to be. I fired three rounds, taking out another that was trying to get at the two women from the right side. I turned back at the pack in front and saw one loping at me. I sent two more rounds flying, but both impacted its shoulder. While I could see it visibly recoil, it sure as shit did not stop it in its tracks. Just as it reached me, I moved to the side, trying to avoid the creature. It half worked. It reached out with its arm and pulled me towards it as it fell forward, successfully bringing me to the ground. I punched it repeatedly in the head, but to no avail. I screamed in agony as I felt intense pain as its teeth bit into my arm. Blood visibly fell from the mouth of the infected as I was finally able to pull my knife up and plunged it into its eye socket. It went limp on top of me. "Shepherd!" I heard from a ways back, most likely Rachel having heard me go down. "Oh fuck oh fuck," I said to myself as I pulled the infected off of me and stared down at my bleeding wound. At that moment, the entire world stopped. My eyes traced over each inch of broken skin; the tooth marks plainly visible. "I'm infected," I whispered to myself. Tears formed in my eyes as I realized that I was going to die, and not only that but in the absolute worst way. Turning into one of those things was a horrific way to die. It would start with a fever, then a sharp pain in my gut, to the point where it would feel like I had a glass ball with spikes inside my stomach. It would be excruciating. Shortly after, the fever would come back in full force and boil what was left of my brain as I lay unable to do a thing about it. Then I'd turn, into one of those walking nightmares. Would my soul be trapped in that body? Or would I be able to go to the gates once the real me stopped breathing? The world began to speed back up as I heard the sound of gunfire dissipate and knew that the crew would be helping me up in no time. I stood and bolted for the Humvee beside me, sitting down in the driver seat and pulling a medical kit from the passenger floorboard. I quickly dressed the wound, covering the bloody wound as best that I could. I pulled the sleeve down on my fatigue top, covering the bite wound with it, and pulled my other arm sleeve down to match. "Is everyone okay?" I heard Ashmore shout from the back side of the Humvee. "Everyone sound off!" Rachel shouted. One by one I heard everyone do so. When I was the only one that did not, I heard Rachel yell again for me. She was coming for me fast.

"I'm okay!" I shouted out of the open door, a lump beginning to form in my throat. What had been feet pounding turned back to the sound of feet walking as they approached. I stood up, vacated the vehicle and proceeded to throw up what little I had eaten that morning. "Are you okay?" Rachel asked as she finally located me. "Yeah," I told her as I spit out some more bile. "The fucker got too close for comfort is all," I told her as she looked down at the corpse below us. "Yeah, no kidding," she said, pulling the knife from its eye. She wiped it off on the infected's shirt and handed it back to me. I grabbed it with my right arm, making sure to keep my left arm looking as natural as possible. I placed it back its scabbard. She went from looking at the infected at my feet to the dozen or so around my Humvee. "That was really close," she said to me as she surveyed the bodies. "We should go before more show up," I told her, briskly standing and reentering the Humvee. I opened the door and jumped in, pulling my rifle up and pulling the magazine from it. I had had one round left in the rifle. For a moment, I thought long and hard about just putting it to my chin and pulling the trigger. Instead, I ejected the almost empty magazine, placing it in my pack and fished out another full one. I placed it in the rifle and pulled the charging handle, readying the weapon for the next encounter which I knew was sure to come. Doors began to open and close around me. I just sat in the driver's seat, staring straight ahead. "Are you alright?" she asked me quietly as I felt a hand on my right arm. I couldn't help it, I flinched, feeling fear of her touching me well up in just a moment's time. She recoiled, pulling her hand away. I looked at her, into those gorgeous eyes and as I stared into them, I made the decision. I would not tell her about the bite. At least not yet. She would immediately make us go back to base and what would they do? They'd probably stop me at the gate and have me shot. If not, they'd run all kinds of tests and use me like some lab rat. That is not what I wanted for myself now. I was going to fulfill this mission to the best of my ability. When the time came, I'd tell her, and I'd pull the trigger so no one else would have to bear the guilt of it. I'd handle it. I looked away, back out to the small sea of cars. "Sorry. I'm just a bit shaken up," I told her as I pulled the Humvee into gear. I don't think she bought it but she didn't ask me again. We were able to find a way around the mess of cars, through a row of front yards with very flimsy fences. In short order, we were back on the road. What a way to spend my last few days in life. Then again, I thought to myself, *isn't saving others worthy of such time spent?* To me, this trip meant the ultimate sacrifice. I was going to save those kids and anyone else that I could, even if it killed me.

Chapter Nine: Atencio's Story

We continued on our planned path. I knew this trip would take hours, even in pre-zombapoc, it would have been one of those car rides that a majority of parents would despise taking with their kids. The ones where there isn't a lot of scenery along the way and the kids get bored way too quickly. Unless they have technology at their fingertips the whole ride, they'd be at each other's throats in no time. Although I enjoyed peace and quiet as much as the next guy, I decided to strike up a conversation as we drove on, trying desperately to get my mind off of my upcoming death. "So Atencio, what's your story?" I asked her, pulling everyone out of their own thoughts. For a moment, I thought that she was perhaps asleep, as there was no response to my inquiry. After a few minutes though, she spoke up. "What do you mean?" she asked frankly. "I meant, where are you from? What did you do before? All of that jazz?" I asked her. Another few minutes went by in silence. I thought for sure that she wasn't going to answer and was about to give up and resort to debating where was the best place to shoot myself to minimize the risk of me surviving and becoming a walking enemy of humanity. "I was born in Albuquerque, and I'm twenty years old," she said. I personally thought that was a weird choice to start it off with but who am I to judge." She continued on, "My life growing up was like everyone else's I guess. Maybe not though, because my family was all pure New Mexican. My entire family was born and raised here and like any true New Mexican family, we always kept an entire freezer in our garage fully stocked with different strains of green and red chili. We had cans of the stuff and my family made their own sauces." "No shit?" I asked her, glancing back at her. My mouth was starting to water at the thought of it. *Anyone who had never experienced New Mexican culture before the fall missed out big time*, I thought to myself as I turned back and looked out the windshield. *Nothing was better than sitting down at a local Mexican restaurant, ordering*

Huevos Rancheros, with Christmas. Not sure what that is? Then your bucket list missed out before the zombapoc, and I am so fricken sorry. "No shit," she said, interrupting my inner diatribe. Another few moments went by, maybe so she could muster her thoughts. "I grew up towards the higher-end of the income level. I know I had it better than most kids my age. The best schools, a phone really early on, and I never truly went without. Once I got old enough to start working, I realized just how shitty life was for most people. I took so much for granted. I used to not even give a poor person a second glance. Now, here we are. All of us, rich or poor only by our own definitions." "I think what he was actually asking was more like where you were when the world stopped as opposed to your entire life story," Ashmore said from beside her. "Oh," Atencio said, realizing just how much more sense that made. "No, it's fine. Continue please, you're helping keep me awake," I told her quickly, reassuring her. "Okay well. I'll fast forward a bit," she said, taking a few more minutes. Rachel in the passenger seat had apparently fallen asleep. *Lucky woman,* I thought as I watched her head roll from side to side with movement of the vehicle. Damn, she was beautiful. "I was working at an ice cream place when it all went down," she said. Fuck, now she was talking about ice cream. I felt my stomach rumble as I patted it with my left hand, as if to say calm down there buddy. "I was one of those preppy girls that all of their friends drop by for free ice cream. The company could afford it and I was their best employee after all," she said. I saw Ashmore visibly roll her eyes as she looked out of the passenger side window. A grin came across my face as I continued to listen, but the grin was unfortunately short-lived. "You'd think with all of that money, we would have been more prepared," she said, shaking her head. "We didn't have bars on our windows or barbed wire on our fences. Those kinds of things just didn't add property value," she said with a hint of disgust. "When they came, we had no real weapons either. They broke in all over the house. I could hear them all through the house, knocking things over, destroying whatever was in their path. My family and I ran upstairs and tried to hide. It didn't last though. I don't know if they smelled us or just happened upon us. Eventually, they figured out where we were. We were in my parent's room in the second floor. They began banging on the door, the hinges shaking with every strike. My father had us go to the window of the bedroom. It was almost a sheer drop, with nothing but a small set of bushes to break our fall. It was just me, my mom and my dad. He was lowering me down using a sheet when the zombies finally broke through the door. I heard my mom scream and felt myself begin to fall. I hit the ground hard, my dad having let completely go of the sheet. I looked up and saw my mom trying to get out of the window. I heard my dad fighting to hold them off as she did. I heard him scream and saw her as she let go from the window seal. At the last possible moment, an arm reached out and grabbed her. Then another, and another. They had her by the shirt and the arm. I don't know how many of them there were. They pulled her back in, as she screamed and fought with every ounce of her being. It didn't help. She yelled for me to run before they bit into her." Her voice was shaking now, as if watching the whole event unfold in her mind. The memories being conjured up like a horror movie. "So, I ran. I ended up finding a group of soldiers on their way here to Cannon and hitched a ride. I joined the first chance that I got. Anything that I could do to kill as many of those fuckers as possible," she said, a look of determination now etched on her face. "I'm sorry," I told her genuinely. "We all have our burdens to bear," she said, and went back to looking out of the hummer's driver side window.

There were no truer words than those, I thought to myself as we drove along. That woman was a true fighter and on the early side of her twenties to boot. She was as sassy as they came, stunningly gorgeous and although she was quite short, her attitude more than made up for it. I started to grin, and received another nudge from Rachel. I didn't even realize that she had woken up. Maybe her women's man thought radar went off, who knows? Her right eyebrow had an upward tilt to it as if she was somehow reading my thoughts. I dropped my grin as quickly as I could and coughed as if that would somehow fix it. She stared at me long and hard, as if marking my soul for transport to hell. Women are scary. Eventually though, she looked away and back out her own passenger window. The amount of pure relief that I felt as she finally moved her eyes away from me was palpable. It was an enormous weight lifted off of my shoulders. I could keep going with the descriptors but I bet you get it. I knew exactly what mistake not to make in the future. I'm not knocking Rachel at all; she is stunningly beautiful. More on the petite side though, and even though she kept her hair usually in a braid, she was as feminine and beautiful as ever. She could sport jeans and a t-shirt with no problem and hopefully soon, a flowing white wedding dress. I stared at her for long moments, feeling my emotions going from happiness at picturing her with her hair down, and her in a white dress to realizing that I was already nearing the end of my short life. I'd never get to experience that happiness that I so truly desired, and because of my mistake, neither would she. I had not only doomed my hopes and dreams, but hers as well. I looked away, and tilted my head away from her so she wouldn't see the tears forming in my eyes. *This so fucking sucks*, I thought as we drove on, my eyes fixing on the dust-covered open road ahead of us, moving ever forward.

Chapter Ten: Ashmore's Story

Another dozen or so miles flew by of which had passed in silence. I was actually starting to doze off as a new voice spoke up. "My Dad worked graveyards, and was away when they came to my house," Ashmore, the medic spoke up. My first thought was, *are we really going to travel down depression lane a second time in an hour?* My second was, *I wonder what happened.* She continued, without a moment's hesitation. "I had been doing clinicals and job shadowing EMTs the week everything went to shit." She paused briefly and then continued; "I saw over and over these people turning into those things. Even with the National Guard being called into the hospital where we were bringing patients, it didn't seem to matter. We were flooded with emergency calls. It was absolute chaos. It wasn't until we started getting swarmed by those things that we finally realized that there was nothing further that we could do to help. Three of us in one ambulance trying to make our way out through that shit fest," she said, her head shaking back and forth now. "Then what happened?" Rachel asked quietly, nudging her forward in her narrative. It worked. "We tried to follow the military instructions of a safety point at the community college, but we got there too late too. The whole place was a raging firefight. The military was trying their damndest to hold the parking lot but between the civis trying to jump into the Evac trucks, and the sheer number of infected converging on them, it was just a matter of time. There were points when soldiers were just firing into crowds, not caring if they hit the living or the dead, just trying to keep the hordes away. This wasn't always the case. For every one panicking soldier, there were five with a good head on their soldiers, trying to keep things moving the right way. In the end, it didn't matter though. Only a handful of trucks made it out of the Evac zone before it fell. It was a bloodbath. We saw the writing on the wall and tried to just bail. Kind of hard to though when you run out of gas." She paused again, looking back at Rachel. "The three of us walked for hours before we realized one of us was bitten. He damn near got us in our sleep. We found shelter in an abandoned van along route 66. I woke up that day to my friend trying to eat my other friend. I had to beat the bitten friend's head in. That was the only training they gave us to defend ourselves. Aim for the head. For fuck sake, I knew both of their families." The tears were coming down hard now, and though she tried to contain them, she broke down. Atencio leaned over to hug her, a gesture that Ashmore readily accepted. "I was the only one to make it to Cannon. After that with my limited medical knowledge, I was put through as a medic. I don't know what happened to my family. I never heard from them again, and no one that I had known my whole life made it to Cannon," she said through sobs. I drove along silently, letting her get it out. In this shitty apocalypse, we all have to release our burdens sometime or just fall apart. Man card or not, if you weren't in touch with your emotions during this era of survival, you probably weren't meant to survive. We as humans can only hold so much inside of us before we snap. It's one of the reasons why they did everything that they could back at base to keep morale up. Those that had nothing to live for would just cease to live, either by taking themselves out or in some documented cases, they just stopped breathing in their sleep. The human body is an amazing thing, capable of incredible feats of strength but it's only as strong as a person's will. Where there's a will, there's a way.

It wasn't long before we came upon yet another blockade of vehicles. As we came to a stop before the closest line of cars, I put the Humvee in park. Kenneth led the team through the mess of cars on foot, looking for the easiest path through. They also kept an eye out for any diesel vehicles that they could syphon fuel from. It wasn't a large haul of fuel by any means, but it would help shore up our supply. While they moved forward, Rachel and I stayed back with the convoy. I asked her to keep a lookout while I changed out of my blood-stained, fatigue cover and into a fresh one. Having a dirty shirt on didn't bother me one bit, however, having a clean one would make hiding my fatal wound that much easier. It took us two hours to move cars out of the way to skirt through that barrel of fun. This time around, not one infected made an appearance. Hopefully, this was a sign of what was yet to come; our mission getting easier. I doubted it though. One of my colloquialisms was that 'Life is funny. Not funny like ha ha, but ironic and full of plot twists.' I had a feeling deep inside that most of us would perish on this mission. Too much could go wrong and it's not hard to imagine the incredibly wide variety of ways that we could meet our end. Falling down a cliff, stepping on a nail and getting an infection, getting struck by lightning, being eaten by a ravenous group of lose wild dogs, the possibilities were damn near endless. We finally drove through the newly created path and I noticed in my rear view mirror a storm forming behind us. New Mexico is well known to residents and aviators alike for the incredible thunderstorms that spawned here. I just knew as I stared back at the dark clouds that they would head our way, because why the hell not. The question was, where would we be when it finally caught up with us? I put my foot down a little harder on the accelerator as we drove onward, hoping to not be on the road when the clouds finally took a dump on us.

Chapter Eleven

We passed through the town of Vaughn without a hitch. We still had not seen neither hide nor hair of anyone, undead or otherwise. When we made it into Encino, New Mexico though, our relatively positive outlook quickly changed. Just as we came to what had appeared to have once been a mechanic shop, a rifle round dinged off of the hood of my vehicle. I slammed on the breaks, and this time, Kenneth did not have enough time to react. He slammed into the rear of my Humvee, causing a case of whiplash that I really did not want or need right just then. I looked around as quickly as I could and surveyed the occupants. Everyone was fine, minus some pain from the immediate stoppage. I recovered from the disorientation of the nudge of the other Humvee and I threw mine into reverse and yelled out of my window, "Back the fuck up!" Ken must have heard me as I saw him glance down at the gearbox, then look backwards as his vehicle began to move away. Another two rounds made their way up the hood of my Humvee, and a third put a neat round hole into the windshield. Thank our lucky stars or whatever deity you may believe in, but it passed harmlessly through the vehicle. Kenneth must have finally figured out that we were under some serious fire as we were both now in full reverse, nearly attached, grill to rear. When we were out of firing range, I lightly hit the brakes several times, hopefully signaling that it was clear. We came to an abrupt stop, and all of our group stepped out from our seats. The damage had been minimal, as these beasts were made to handle almost everything. Whoever took a shot at us though was now at the top of my list for people that I disliked and any hopes of them receiving the other half of a best friend's forever necklace from me were completely dashed. "We've got two options. We go around them, or we go through them," I said calmly once everyone had settled down, the adrenaline that had built up dissipating. The weather had a cool breeze flowing by, rustling all of our clothes and the ladies hair while we stood. "We need to hurry the fuck up and get to Albuquerque," Rachel said, "We're already far behind schedule." I nodded in agreement. "That's my thought as well. Anyone else have any ideas?" I asked, looking at each person in turn. Atencio spoke up, "They shot at us without even a moment's hesitation. I say fuck them," she said, the ever-present fire in her eyes. "Maybe they thought we were hostile?" Jaylin asked the team quietly. "They didn't give us a warning shot, or anything else to give us a chance to let them know that we weren't. If they thought we were, odds are they think everyone is," Ashmore piped in. "If they shot at us so quickly, I can only imagine their response to refugees trying to make it to Cannon and attempting to pass through here," Atencio said. "Alright. That sounds like a consensus. Everyone get prepped for a firefight. Hopefully, we won't need to fire a shot but if that changes, weapons free." Nods came from all around the group. I stood for an extra moment, closing my eyes and inhaling deeply. I was attempting to mentally prepare myself for the upcoming battle. Killing zombies and even their infected by not undead counterparts are one thing. Killing other human beings, especially with the world the way it was now where every life was precious did not sit well with me. Unfortunately, I doubted that they'd just flag us down and apologize for shooting at us, and I wouldn't allow those in our group to get hurt because of some assholes not liking us driving through their town. The cool breeze felt invigorating on my skin as I slowly shook my head, letting those thoughts dissipate as I turned and walked back to the Humvee. Everyone else had already filed back into our vehicles and every window minus one had rifles pointing outwards as we began to roll forward. It's far too difficult to aim and shoot a rifle out of an open window while driving in my case. Difficult, but not impossible as countless road signs around small towns can attest to. The bullet hole in the windshield was not large which led me to believe it was not a very high caliber round and so the distance from the shooter to the Humvee when it was hit must not have been very far. I told everyone in my vehicle to keep as low of a profile as possible, and as we once again came up to the mechanic shop, rounds began to pepper my bumper. I swerved, in an attempt to relieve some of the stress for the Humvee. As I moved the wheel to the right, I saw flashes of light coming from atop a small building on the right. A small-town post office sat, with two pickup trucks in the parking lot, turned sideways. I pointed to Rachel who was still in the front passenger seat. "Up there!" I shouted. She followed my gaze and started firing rounds in that direction. The shooter, an obvious amateur stood up to continue firing at us. After giving up his only cover, it didn't take long for Rachel's bullets to trace up the building and to stitch him along his button up shirt buttons. He fell hard onto the old cracked concrete on the ground level of the post office. If this had been a cartoon, I have no doubt that landing would have been accompanied by a splat sound effect. I had to give the woman props, even with the gunfight raging, she didn't flinch as rounds hit our vehicle repeatedly. Her rifle danced from target to target, firing short bursts and eliminating each threat one by one. Two more men opened up on us by the pickup trucks as we passed, peppering the side of our ride. We returned fire like an old-fashioned ship to ship cannon battle and as I glanced to my right,

I saw another go down. I heard a yelp of pain as we pulled past the small makeshift barricade. Kenneth was directly behind me and much to the chagrin of the shooter on our right who was still trying to take us out, Isabel pulled even with him and put a well-placed shot directly into the man's head as he turned to bring his rifle to bare on their vehicle. Kenneth then sped up to get back onto our tail. I knew someone was hit but I couldn't tell who and I didn't have the time to figure it out. People seemed to pop out of everywhere, damn near out of nearby bushes. As Kenneth and I drove on, keeping our heads down, the women around us continued to pour lead into our attackers. I felt one and then two of our tires pop and deflate. Most Humvees are fitted with run flat tires, and they allow the vehicles to continue to operate albeit at a reduced speed without locking up the axles. It took a lot of work on my end to hold the wheel steady as the run flats did their work. We weren't hauling ass through the town originally but now we were even slower, and the amount of fire that we were taking was insane. For a small town during a zombapoc, there were a crap ton of these aggressors. I honestly hadn't thought that there were this many people left alive outside of our gates in the state. Another yelp from my right almost had me hit the brakes. Rachel was to my right. *No no no no* I repeated to myself as I slammed down on the accelerator as hard as I could, nearly standing on it, trying to get out of this death trap. We finally passed out of the range of the shooters in the town and out of the city limits. I drove another two miles before pulling over. Kenneth didn't miss a beat as he pulled in behind me. I jumped out and immediately went for Rachel's door. It was already open. Ashmore was tending to her before I even made it to her. I had to give it to her, she was fast. I was not a slouch either as I came to her. The bullet had grazed her shoulder and she was bleeding. "Baby, are you okay?" I asked her, worry evident in my voice. "She's fine, chill," Ashmore said to me, not interested at all in my attempts to get in her way. "Sorry," I said, but still completely in her way. She physically pushed me backwards. "Back the hell up, I'm trying to work!" she said. The look in her eyes told me to start treading very lightly. I stayed back and watched intently as she applied a small bandage to the wound. It was not bad by any means but if you've ever been in love, you'd know that even a stubbed toe is enough to be concerned about with your significant other. Ashmore stepped to the side and Rachel finally stood from the Humvee and embraced me and I hugged the hell out of her while trying hard to avoid the wound. I then snapped. "Oh my God, who else got hit?" I damn near shouted. "It was me and I'm fine," Atencio was behind me, watching the whole spectacle. A fresh burn mark ran along her cheek. "Holy shit," I said as I looked over at her. Ashmore applied some ointment to her cheek and that was about it. "Yeah, a little more to the left and I'd be dead," Atencio said. "Just like that?" I asked, a bit surprised that she was so nonplussed about it. She shrugged. "I'm not dead and chicks dig scars," she said. My eyebrow raised at that a little bit, but I didn't have time to ponder that whole bag of whatever that was about. I let go of my fiancé and ran to the Humvee behind us. All three of those occupants were standing around and in completely good health. Our vehicle had apparently taken the brunt of what the town had to offer and for once, I was totally okay with being the guinea pig. We survived and no one was seriously injured. It was a damned miracle. I swore though that if one of us got back to Cannon, we'd have them bomb the whole damn town somehow. *Fuck those guys*, I thought as we spent the time to replace not one but two fricken tires. Afterwards, we piled back into our vehicles and once again set out on the long road ahead, hopeful that the next town would be a bit more welcoming.

Chapter Twelve

The gas station at Clines Corners was completely dry, which was quite unfortunate, if I do say so myself. We had enough fuel to make it to Albuquerque, but anyone left alive these days could tell you that it's always best to top off the tanks whenever possible. You never really know where you'll be when the gauge hits E. We repeatedly stopped to syphon fuel tanks from other trucks along our route with the abandoned semis generally having the greatest yields.. Every stop had us on edge and that, naturally, wore us out. The human body can only take so much and all the adrenaline over the course of the past twelve hours or so was almost too much. Everyone in the convoy was exhausted. I began to see locales that I could remember from my previous trek in the opposite direction. I had narrowly escaped Albuquerque with

Sergeant Steven Rodriguez. I carried the memory of that brave man in my heart wherever I went. He and I had made the trip together all of the way to Cannon and he had been like a brother to me. All good things must come to an end as they say and I lost my brother to the horde attack at Cannon just after we arrived. Putting a bullet in him was the thing that single-handedly haunted me the most in my memories and my dreams and even in this apocalyptic wasteland and with a mighty high zombie kill count, that's saying something. It is different though pulling the trigger on someone that you knew. Even worse when it's family or a dear friend. *This world sucks*, I thought as I drove on, slowing to move around the obstacles littering the roadway. Two more hours and we reached the Albuquerque city limits. The path had previously been mostly cleared by the sheer numbers of infected following in our wake out of the city. They had pushed cars aside and off of the main road as they stretched out. Soon, our Humvee rode over the final hill leading into Albuquerque, we saw it once again loom large in front of us. I had made this trip a dozen or so times. Albuquerque had previously been my home of around 15 years, and each trip, seeing Abq over the hill, it had been an absolute relief. To know that I was almost home. Now though, it was an empty shell of what it had once been. No city lights greeted us this time and no traffic driving just a little too fast without using their blinkers. As we came upon yet another roadblock, this one past the Tramway Boulevard exit, but before the Juan Tabo exit. I decided that it was time for us to figure out our next move. I parked at the leading edge of the car pile and Kenneth pulled up beside me. The ladies were all asleep. Kenneth and I stood, surveying the interstate in front of us. "I think we should backtrack and find a safe place to sleep," Kenneth told me. I eventually nodded and sighed, stretching as I did so. "If the kids have lasted this long, then I doubt one more day will make much of a difference. We being dead on our feet though won't help matters at all," I replied, looking back at the other man. His eyes were bloodshot, probably as much as mine were. He nodded and we shuffled back to our vehicles. He pulled out ahead of me and I followed his lead. We made our way back onto the Tramway exit, ignoring the wrong way signs and found a local motel within eyesight of the interstate. We woke everyone and cleared the rooms with ease. Not a single living infected remained, or undead for that matter in the building. Rachel and I bunked together with Isabel and Kenneth doing the same. Jaylin, Atencio and Ashmore got the room next to ours. With all of our doors firmly locked, and our rifles nearby and ready for action, we all passed into the realm of deep sleep. As if on cue, a dream began to roll in my mind, like that of an old-fashioned movie projector. I hoped for all that I was worth, that it was just a dream and not some kind of vision.

The dream began like most others, or at least I thought so. Rachel and I were sitting in chairs along some unnamed beach. Our hands were intertwined and as I glanced over, I saw her in a bikini. *It was going to be one of those dreams*, I thought, marveling in the absolute beauty of her female figure. If you're a man, you know what I'm talking about. Then again; Ladies, you probably have similar dreams just with less cheesy fantasy types. Who knows, maybe y'all are as goofy in your dreams as we are. I blinked, enjoying the scenery. The sand on the beach began to swirl into the air, causing me to try to cover my eyes from the assault. The wind picked up as if a storm was moving ashore. Dark clouds seemed to arrive quicker than I think I had ever seen clouds move in all of my years. I looked at my fiancé and the longer that I stared at her, the more distant she seemed to become. In a split instant, I saw her move impossibly fast, still in her chair and now far enough that I could no longer see her. My hand outstretched as if I could somehow reach out to grab her. The world around me turned into what felt like the center of hurricane. A storm raged all around me and I was alone. The cold feeling of rain swept over me and suddenly, a rifle was in my hand, and I was firing into a mass of infected. They were building up, creating an undead ramp up to the top floor of the building that I stood upon. Above me was a helicopter, its propellers kicking up dust all around me. I looked up at it, and saw several children boarding, with Rachel ushering them into the waiting bird. Kenneth was beside me, matching me round for round. I yelled at him to board the black hawk. He didn’t. Maybe he hadn't heard me, so I pointed and shouted again. "Get on the fucking chopper!" He didn't move or acknowledge me in anyway. I ran towards him just as the infected made the rooftop. As I watched, the crowd of undead avalanched straight towards him. He screamed. Oh God, did he scream as they swarmed over him. I pulled my trigger with every fiber of my being, screaming my own scream of pain and anguish as I pushed forward, popping heads as I went. "No!" I yelled as I neared the pile of corpses in front of me. His bloody lifeless face peered up at me, with a look of sheer terror still etched on it. I heard another scream and looked up. The infected had made it to the helicopter. *How?!* I yelled in my head as I ran towards my love. It was pointless. Like the devil's personal flood of bodies, it rose and pulled the helicopter down. My fiancé, my only reason for living was enveloped in the horde. I fired every round that I had left in my magazine but it was useless. As the black hawk crashed to the ground, a fiery mess of destruction rained down around me. I dropped my rifle as I was consumed by grief. "No no no," I repeated to myself, hitting the ground on my knees. All of the noise; the explosions and the moans of the infected stopped in that instant. As I realized that it was pure quiet, I looked up, the tears rolling down my cheeks in full force. All of the zombies had crowded around me and were staring at me hungrily. As I turned my head from side to side, I saw everyone that I knew. There was Kenneth, freshly risen. Isabel, Atencio and Jaylin off to my right. Ashmore to my left, still holding her medical bag. Directly in front was Rachel, dressed in a wedding gown. *Oh God,* I thought as they all lunged at me at once. *Fitting*, I thought as I stood and lifted my arms, ready to go willingly into the afterlife. I felt the first set of teeth tear into me and I screamed.

Chapter Thirteen

My scream carried over into life as I screamed out in my sleep. Rachel was immediately shaking me out of my nightmare. It took a few moments as my eyes finally opened and I stared up at her, tears still streaming down my face. I hugged her as hard as she could take, and I didn't want to let her go. She rubbed her fingers through my hair and along the skin of my back, trying whatever she could to comfort me. I heard a knock on the door to the room. Rachel shouted, "He's fine, everything's okay," to whomever came to check on us. I still couldn't speak and just kept my head buried into my fiancé's arms. Like the amazing woman she is, she didn't budge. Eventually, I passed back into sleep, the exhaustion getting the best of me.

I awoke several hours later, still wrapped in her arms. If the room had been filled with other men, man card policy dictated that I be the one holding her. I'm not a fool though, I know damn well that women are the fairer sex. They are the strongest, and the most cunning. Some men will say what? Strongest, how is that possible? To them, I say, until we squeeze a living child out of us, I don't care how much we can bench press, they're stronger. Which may or may not be good news for men. I learned this very early on in my dating life and have stuck to the knowledge that I will never truly understand what a woman is thinking, or how they really feel. They are a complete mystery, like the black holes eating up whole galaxies in the night sky. Does NASA know what makes them tick? Nope. Do men really know what makes women tick? Not a chance in hell and any man that says otherwise is a goof. As my inner dialogue came to an end, my chivalry came to the forefront as I unwrapped her arms from around me and immediately wrapped her up in mine. I couldn't lay there and not return the favor. For what I estimated as an hour, I watched the beauty sleep, rubbing my own fingers through her hair. When she woke up, she slowly looked up at me. A small grin crept over her face. "How long?" she said simply. "Like 37 years," I responded, a smile forming on my own face. "You've been watching me sleep for 37 years?" she asked. "Yes, and worth every damn minute of it," I said, giving her a light kiss on her forehead. Her smile was now full on. A light tap on the door interrupted our revelry. "Can you two please get dressed so we can go?" a small woman's voice from the other side of the door said loudly. "Nope, you go get em' tiger, we'll stay here and bang each other like a brand-new set of drums on Christmas day," I yelled back. "Cringe," I heard the voice say as they walked away. "We should get up," Rachel said to me, still staring at me. "I wasn't kidding when I said I was going to bang you like a drum," I said, a shit eating grin still plastered on my face. "Not right now Romeo, we've got a job to do." She stood, and stretched. "But!" I stammered out, still holding out hope. She put her index finger to my lips. "Shush. When we get back," she whispered to me as she kissed me passionately. She then turned and began to get dressed. I too got dressed but begrudgingly so. Blue balls be damned. Finally, we were prepped and ready to go. We were the last ones to the Humvees. Awkward was one way to put it when we walked out and everyone was there just staring at us. "That was so good babe. You're the best I ever had. Especially that new elephant position. That was so amazing," I told her loudly, causing her to blush and smack me on the arm. "Eww," Atencio said, getting into the vehicle to avoid hearing anymore. "Shut it, Shep and get in the truck," Rachel told me. We had played this game many times, and it was never not fun for either of us. I did as I was told though and within a few moments, we were back on our merry way. The clouds had caught up with us and even though the sun should have been rising soon, I knew that the storm would envelope the sky sooner rather than later and we'd be lucky for even one ray of sunshine today. We made our way slowly down the main road of Albuquerque, Central Ave. also known as Route 66 towards our destination.

Speaking of which. "Where are we going again?" I asked Rachel who had once again been seated to my right. "Are you serious?" she asked me, a bit miffed. "No, not at all, I was just joking," I said with a short burst of nervous laughter. She put her head in her hands and let out a rather large exasperated sigh. "We are going to Monte Vista Elementary School to hopefully rescue some kids, remember?" she said matter of factly. "Right, Right, of course," I said, nodding in response. From out of the corner of my eye, I could see her still shaking her head. "Wow," I heard from behind me as Atencio spoke up. "He's a real keeper," she said with a little laugh. "No kidding," Ashmore said off to her right. "Thanks, peanut gallery," I said, now a bit flustered, the heat of embarrassment rising up my neck to my cheeks. "You can't expect me to remember every little thing. I have a whole lot of other things going on in my head," I said, trying to defend myself. "Nope, we just expect you to remember the one important thing," Ashmore said. The two women in the back seats high-fived each other. I took a deep breath and let it roll off of my back, or tried to. Men's egos are easily bruised but the bruises tend to become easily forgotten, especially with me. It was maybe two minutes tops before my mind began to wander to some really weird places. Would zombies eat people if they were covered in extra hot green chili? Would it confuse the undead at all, or just make the person an even tastier snack? Could zombies become as addicted to chili as us New Mexicans have become? How much I missed it. I'm sure I was drooling as I drove. No one mentioned it though as we slowly moved past burnt husks of cars and buildings, assorted piles of long dead and rotting corpses in the road, and even passed one running infected. I suppose we had attracted her by the sound of our vehicles and she must have been damn near a track star in her previous life. She stayed almost on our rear bumper for three blocks before we began to pull away. She would have overtaken us with no problem had we been on foot. I thanked our lucky stars that we still had two working vehicles. The apocalypse had a way of trimming us all down in a way that only those with limited rations could be. We weren't starving by any means, but I was not enjoying my weekly two breakfast burritos each Wednesday either. On the plus side, we were all far leaner and fit than any of us had ever been before. Not to toot my own horn, but I looked pretty amazing. Dare I say hot? That thought though quickly went from a jovial one to that of despair as I thought about the wound on my arm that even then was throbbing slightly. I quickly shut down that thought train real quick, and refocused on the road ahead.

Monte Vista was off of Central Avenue just a block or so up from the University of New Mexico. The area had been heavily populated and we had attempted to clear the area of supplies several times during our previous stay here but never had really succeeded. Not too far away was UNM Hospital and a huge area of residential homes, not including the university's own dorms. Unfortunately, that meant a near constant trickle of infected during our runs here. *This was going to be an exciting trip,* I thought to myself. *Then again, it had already been, hadn't it?* The bite wound on my arm began to itch, and as I drove, I tried repeatedly to scratch it without actually scratching at it. If you've ever had a bug bite or chicken pox, or even poison ivy, you know what I mean. We moved along Central in the west bound lane and oddly enough, only that one single infected had been seen since entering Abq. My best guess was that we had taken a majority of them with us out of the city on our initial escape. As we continued onwards, I kept my speed down, not only for the obvious risks of debris in the road but just looking around the area. This place had been my home, and the home for all of my crew. I had moved from place to place in the city somewhere in the vicinity of over a dozen times since arriving in New Mexico. Each move seemed to be in a different part of the city. Each area had their pros and cons, of that I was certain of. I spotted very familiar restaurants and stores that I had visited repeatedly over my tenure. A case of nostalgia swept over me like a tidal wave. We made it to our destination with no issues at all. Frankly, it was absolutely eerie for things to go right for once.

Turning off of Route 66, and past a long-abandoned police substation, we spotted the school. In a city saturated with old Spanish and southwestern style architecture, it was clear to see this building was not any of that sort. Built in 1931, it was much more Mediterranean design than any other building in the area. Considering how long it had been standing, it seemed well up kept. Parking spots lined the road along a sidewalk to the east side, and small parking areas behind and in front of the school sat, with dust and dirt piled up like drifts of snow up against several still sitting vehicles. One thing that we did notice, however, was a recently used foot trail leading from the main doors of the school out to the street. "What's the plan?" Rachel asked me as we pulled up into the parking spots. "Hold on," I told her, as I backed up the Humvee, corrected my alignment and then parked perfectly within the lines, taking two tries to get it right. "Sorry, what did you say?" I asked her, glancing over. She was, of course, just staring at me. "Did you just fix your parking?" she asked. "Well yeah, it was embarrassing. I have standards," I told her, looking at her confused. "Wow, you really picked the brightest bulb in the shed, didn't you?" Ashmore asked as she got out. Rachel visibly sighed and also vacated the vehicle. Kenneth had pulled in next to us on my driver side and had also made sure to correctly align into the spots. We fist bumped each other on exiting and commented about just how well each of us parked, pointing and even moving some of the dust along the parking spot lines away with our feet. "And that's why I only like women," Atencio said as she shouldered her rifle and looked up at the school looming before us. "Me too," said Ashmore as she stood beside her. Kenneth and my conversation died on our lips and we stood and looked at the two women. "You both?" Kenneth asked. Ashmore gave Atencio a quick peck on the cheek and they walked forward up the dead lawn of the school. It was safe to say that we were dumbstruck. Guys are generally oblivious that way. "Come on boys," Rachel said, with Isabel right behind her. Jaylin elected to stay with the vehicles, keeping them guarded in case we had to make a hasty exit. We did as we were told and followed close behind. The two mean women led the way, and pulled the large wooden doors open. They swung open with a loud screech as the rusted hinges protested the movement. All of our flashlights turned on and the ladies scanned the interior. Nothing jumped out at them. Atencio and Ashmore then went left and cleared the office, the remaining three of us went to the right and moved down the dark corridor. A locked nurses' room to the immediate right was locked, so we moved on quickly. We cleared a technology room and what looked to be a teachers' break room. I looked back and saw the other two women continue to the left, and they began to clear a kindergarten room and the adjourning classrooms. We cleared the entirety of the main school building and came across absolutely nothing. There was no sign of infected or anyone living for that matter. As we began to walk back towards the entrance, I happened to pass a door that led outside to what I guessed was the playground. Not far in the distance though, I saw what looked to be a set of mobile classrooms. In one window, what had to have been a flickering light of some kind caught my eye. I wished right then that I could whistle. I was, unfortunately, one of those people that had never grasped the concept of being able to whistle though and instead, shouted as quietly as I could, "Psssst." It worked though as the crew gathered around me to see what I was seeing. We, unfortunately, did not all fit in the window frame enough to all look at once, so I was pushed to the rear as everyone else looked on. Eventually, everyone spotted our goal. Like a kid chosen to lead the class to the lunch room, I regained my previous position at the front of the line and opened the exit slowly and everyone filed in behind me. I led the way to the mobile classrooms, and they stacked up behind me on the metal lined ramp leading to the door. The day was turning colder quickly and being outside with the storm brewing above did not help my morale much. My neck and arm hairs began to stand on end as I grabbed the door handle and pulled it open. We moved in as a unit and cleared the small room quickly. While it had once been a classroom, it had obviously been made into a small living area. Old mattresses and blankets were all over the place, with hand painted pictures covering most of the windows. Trash bags of food wrappers and other waste was piled up in one corner, as if someone was saving up for trash day. As our flashlights scanned the interior, in the very far corner sat two extremely frightened children. Granted, each of our rifles was pointed squarely at them and so I had no doubt we were a majority of the cause for their alarm. One by one, we lowered our weapons. Rachel rushed forward, not giving one single fuck about the condition of the children. "Are you two okay?" she said, embracing them into a motherly hug. The two kids began to cry heartily as they embraced her back. The rest of us just kind of stood there, taking in the whole room. The desks had been pushed to the perimeter of the interior of the room, allowing for the children to stand on the desks to peer out the windows. I supposed that they would also use them to barricade the door to the class if they had to. A sink sat along one wall, and several cans of food were stacked beside it. Toys were everywhere, littered around the floor like almost every kid in America's room would be before their parents told them it was time to clean it. Only these kids most likely no longer had parents to tell them to clean it up. Like so many other children, these two were almost guaranteed to be orphans, and that more than anything sucked donkey balls. They'd never again play catch with their fathers, get their hair done with their mothers before prom, or even have one more single family dinner together. I looked away, feeling tears begin to form as I thought of all of what was lost for these small children. After several minutes, their sobs quieted down and Ashmore stepped up to check their vitals. Other than being somewhat malnourished, they were doing just fine. Isabel spoke next. "Where's the other two of you?" The two boys glanced at each other. "Cara and Cayden went to get more stuff," one of them, a small Hispanic boy of maybe 6 years old said. The other boy, slightly older, maybe 8 years old spoke up. "We told them not to, but they did anyway," he said. "What are your names?" Rachel asked. "I'm Joe, this is Raul," the older boy said, pointing first to himself and then to the smaller boy. "So the two that are missing are Cara and Cayden? A boy and a girl?" she asked intently. The boy just nodded. I let out a quiet curse, hopefully not in earshot of the little ones. *Great, another fun adventure coming right up,* I thought as I listened on. "Where did they go?" she asked next. "They went to the Sub," the younger one said. "What the hell is that?" I asked, far louder than I expected to sound. Rachel immediately gave me the 'say another word and die' stare. I, knowing when the fairer sex was right, immediately shut my trap. "Where is the Sub?" she asked, turning her attention back to the boys. "At the university," the older one said. "UNM?" she inquired. Both boys nodded. "Well, grab my ears," Atencio said and I looked over at her with a quizzical look on my face. She saw me look over at her and just smiled, shaking her head. I let it drop, but swore then and there that I would get the rest of that out of her someday. "I know where that is," Kenneth spoke up and all of our attention turned to him. "It's the student union building. They have a computer lab and some local restaurants that were set up in there. It would probably be a great place to scavenge for food and supplies," he said. Isabel nodded and soon, we were all on board. That, however, left the issue of the two kids in front of us. "Alright. Can we load up the kiddos here and head over to the Sub? We'll need to keep these two under guard so nothing happens to them after we leave here. Any volunteers?" I asked. Every hand in the group shot up. "Wow, I'm so glad y'all are willing to back me up in there," I said. Kenneth's hand lowered first. "Sorry bro," he said sheepishly. I shook my head. "Nope, it's fine, the damage is done," I said, turning my back to him. "He is just being super dramatic, he's fine," Rachel said to Ken, rolling her eyes. Kenneth chuckled. I turned to look at her, trying to look as hurt and upset as possible. "Cut it out, we've got work to do." "Fine fine," I said, giving up on my ruse.

The two children gathered up anything that they wanted to bring. We allowed them to bring all that they wanted and made room for their stuff happily. Within thirty minutes, we were on our way to UNM, also known as the University of New Mexico. A sprawling university with smaller buildings scattered all over the place, it had once been a pride and joy of Albuquerque. The go-to place for those seeking higher education. Now though, it was just as dead as the world around it. The Sub building was three-story-tall and situated almost directly between Central and Campus Blvd. We parked along the street to the south of the building. It was eventually decided that Kenneth, Rachel and I would move into the campus to find the missing children. Atencio, Isabel, Jaylin and Ashmore sat in the first Humvee with Raul and Joe and kept a vigilant lookout. We, on the other hand, made our way slowly and somewhat stealthily towards the target building. We still hadn't seen a sign of anyone or anything which was still extremely odd. For a city that had held hundreds of thousands, it was way too quiet. The white doors to the building swung open silently as if the hinges were freshly oiled. We moved as one and breached it.

Inside, we could hear obvious sounds of battle. Not the kind that we were used to at all though. As we moved farther into the dark interior, two children were holding off a dozen or so infected with nothing but homemade spears. I kid you not, pun intended. As I watched in stunned amazement, a zombie lurched for one, the larger and obviously older of the two. The older one stabbed upwards, sending the pointy end through the eye and into the disease-riddled brain of the aggressor. With a pivot, the girl, yes, it was definitely a girl, withdrew the weapon and let the body fall where it did, her hair pulled up in a tight ponytail. Behind her, the younger boy had managed to hit one in the knee hard enough to catch it off balance, and with a kick to said knee, sent it falling backwards onto the ground. The audible crack of bone as it hit the tile floor was just gross. Trained fighters pre-apoc would be hard pressed to have these kinds of results. However, more infected were coming to the party and it was a foregone conclusion that numbers would outweigh skill. Everyone tires and the same can definitely be said for children. Done with watching the spectacle, Rachel fired first, sending a well-placed round into the head of the closest infected to us. This was to clear us a path and to avoid sending bullets near the children. Kenneth and I followed suit, selecting our targets one by one. Our lights danced around like we were trying to play flashlight tag back in the good old days. I almost yelled, 'Tag, you're it!' as I blasted another infected in the face. As we approached the children, they appeared ready to make a run for it, and in the opposite direction. Rachel spoke up quickly, seeing them eyeing an escape route. "We're the good guys. We found your friends at Monte Vista," she shouted as she ran forward. An obvious spark of recognition came across the girl and she grabbed the boy so he wouldn't take off without her. The boy though was still trying to fight the undead around them, lashing out with his spear whenever he could. The girl though had put the pieces together and realized that their battle was just about over. Rachel made it to them, and put her arms around them, as if creating a mom-like shield around them. If force fields were real, moms everywhere had the ability to summon them from another dimension, of that I was sure of as no harm came to any of them as we pulled up short of the trio, putting two rounds into another infected off to the right. We set up a defense perimeter around the group and held our ground. It was eerily quiet as we stood there among the infected bodies littering the floor. "Are you two okay?" Rachel asked the two children. The girl shrugged off her arm. "Yeah, of course, we are," she said defiantly. Rachel held out her hands in a placating manner. "Okay okay. We have your friends in our car. Can we get out of the dark and go see them?" she asked the two kids. The boy nodded readily, but the girl didn't move. "Come on," Rachel said, grasping the boy's hand. He followed her with no hesitation. I heard what sounded like a shriek and turned to see the girl coming straight at me, weapon raised. She completely caught me off guard. I tried desperately to pull my rifle around to see if I could take a shot before she reached me, but she was far too close. *What a way to die,* I told myself as the sharp, pointy, infected blood covered tip flew right past my cheek and I heard a loud popping noise. I stood there, stunned, with her nearly directly in my face. Or at least as best she could at maybe four feet tall. I turned slowly, and saw that she had impaled another zombie through the left eye this time. It had apparently joined the dinner party late and had tried to sneak in a quick bite of yours truly. I gulped audibly as she pulled the weapon free. The undead fell forward and I moved quickly to avoid it falling upon me. It landed with a loud thump in the darkness. The little shit grinned and followed Rachel and the boy out the front doors. I was still standing, shocked. Kenneth walked up to me. "That little girl just saved your ass man," he said with a chuckle. "Hey bro?" I said back to him in reply. "Yeah?" he asked. "We don't speak of this ever again," I said, looking at him straight in the eyes. Have you ever seen someone smile with their eyes? If you don't know what I mean, it's when someone smiles and their eyes squint. Even without looking at their shit eating grin, you can absolutely tell that they are smiling at you. That was him. "Sure. Sure," he said as he walked away from me, heading for the door. "Fucker," I said as I followed him out.

Ashmore, Isabel and Atencio sat in the Humvee quietly with the two children and watched the group of three make their way through the UNM campus towards the target building. "There they go," Isabel said, with a hint of worry in her voice. "They'll be fine," Atencio said as she scanned the area behind the vehicle. "How do you know that?" Isabel asked, turning to her. Atencio turned back to meet her gaze. "Well, if they all die then our job gets infinitely harder and I don't want to deal with that," she said. A grin crept over Isabel's face. "So, basically, they will be okay because you don't want to work harder?" Isabel asked. Atencio smiled and nodded. "Exactly." "Wow," Ashmore piped in, which of course earned daggers from Atencio. The two children were still sitting in the back seat, completely quiet and watching the adult spectacle in front of them. Jaylin had stayed in the other Humvee. It was probably so she could enjoy a little peace and quiet, though she never said why she had moved. The two women, Atencio and Ashmore began to bicker while Isabel and the children watched. A small crashing sound broke the brewing argument faster than someone holding up fresh bacon to a pack of dogs at a dog park. An awkward silence fell over the group as they sat, just waiting for something to happen. Then as if on cue, Jaylin waived her hands to get the other women's attention. It wasn't until one of the children, Joe, spoke up, "I think that lady wants you," he said, pointing as all of the women turned to look at him. They all looked over in unison and witnessed Jaylin making a gun gesture with her hand and pointing to their left. It must have been comical to see everyone in the Humvee turn at the same time to look out the left side of the vehicle. A group of infected were making the way in their direction. Oddly enough, they were not just out in the open and heading for them with arms outstretched. They appeared to be taking cover behind bushes and trees as they advanced towards the group. "That's new," Ashmore said, staring at the incoming threat. "They've been getting smarter," Raul said quietly to the group. "Out of the mouths of babes," Isabel said, flicking her rifle from safe to semi-automatic. "Are we ready to take care of these guys, ladies?" she asked the group of women. The sound of more rifles readying sounded quickly thereafter. "I'm down," Atencio said as she opened the door and stepped out. "I guess we're going now?" Ashmore said, annoyed as she followed her friend out. Out of the corner of Isabel's eye, she could see Jaylin also disembarking. They all raised their rifles and tracked targets. As the first one came out into the open of the sidewalk, it was immediately downed with a headshot. The remaining thirteen or so broke cover and ran towards the soldiers, moving from side to side, trying to avoid the incoming hail of bullets. Unfortunately, these infected running had not been an over dramatization. They rushed the group, as if they were a group of apparently half-starved Americans chasing after the last Whoppers at a Burger King that was closing for good, and the burgers were free. People will do anything for free crap. Rounds began to pop off at an increased rate, some having missed their targets completely. Just as the group had been whittled down to the last remaining infected, the two children in the Humvee screamed. Jaylin spun, having been the furthest away and spotted a second group coming in from their flanks. With a speed that would be hard to replicate, she turned her rifle in the direction of the new group and began to fire. The second group was larger than the first, with some fast ones making up the head of the pack. The first group was eliminated and the other three adults turned to focus their fire on the new group. The runners had pushed Jaylin back to the first Humvee as she retreated, stepping back with each round fired. Two of the infected plastered their faces up against the rear passenger window of the vehicle with the children, who screamed and looked on in terror. They had impacted the vehicle with such force, attempting to get to the canned food that they broke noses and teeth on the window, smearing blood and pieces of human anatomy all across the windows. Licking the glass frantically as if that would somehow allow them a taste of the warm flesh inside. The women, finding a new gear pushed forward, with Atencio jumping up onto the hood and quickly moving to the top of the roof of the Humvee and firing downwards into the waiting heads of the zombie. The other women quickly moved around the vehicle and put down the rest of the infected before them. The intense firefight was over in just minutes but had most likely caused not only emotional but mental damage to everyone involved, especially the kids inside. The fact that now the infected were planning or at least some were using tactics was downright frightening. A slow shuffling old school movie type of zombie was easy to take out in small groups. Even with larger numbers, they could be managed with discipline. Now though, it was evident that something had changed. Granted, the group of non-threatening infected from the few days before had raised red flags, but this was almost a military type of upgrade. With tactics. It would go without saying that they had a new problem on their hands. Imagine an undead army that could think, plan and attack in new and insane ways. Shit, someday it might just be possible that they begin using their own weapons and even start using a toaster. Then what? Humankind will be wild game hunted for the sport of it. Zombie families will rejoice at their undead kids getting their first kills with a hunting rifle at the human preservations or some crap like that. With the humans of the world maintaining only a toehold, it was only a matter of time before they would be wiped out should the infected evolve much farther.

A pile of infected lay just feet from the front bumper of the closest Humvee. The soldiers stood, their rifles at the ready. Not a single sound assailed to their ears after the last one fell. It was eerie to say the least. As they looked on, they saw the group from the Sub heading their way. Behind them, another group of infected was in semi-hot pursuit. "It's time to go!" I shouted out to the group at the Humvees and saw their female faces lose their color. "There's probably a lot of them behind us," I told Kenneth as we took up the rear guard behind the kids. "Probably," he said back to me as we kept up the pace. "Keep moving!" I said, pushing the group onward. As if somehow, those words would make them run even faster. It's one of those things where do you really need to be told to swim faster when there are sharks coming straight for you? Probably not, but it doesn't hurt to say so. The women in front of us moved several bodies out of the way and cleared a path for us. Bodies were dragged unceremoniously out of the way haphazardly and then the ladies all piled into the rear vehicle, leaving us the closest. We filed in, throwing the children, not so nicely into the rear seats as we did so. Rachel and I slammed our doors closed just as undead finger tips grasped for the opening. As the door locked shut, I was rewarded with at least three fingertips on my lap. To say that it was gross was an absolute understatement. For a moment, I just looked down and stared at them, as if they were a new insanely cool toy set from Toys R US, had they still been in business. Rachel slapped my arm hard, and that broke me out of my trance. I shook the disgusting things off of me and started the engine. Zombies were all around us, pounding with all the excitement you'd expect. Books and movies though do not do the feeling of watching all of those hands pound against your window, trying to get through it with the one goal of eating your flesh. As I moved the vehicle into reverse and began to run over the infected, the kids and adults alike were subject to one of the worst bouncy rides of our lives. We jostled around like popcorn in a movie theater cooker. It was both fun and absolutely terrifying at the same time. Fun because being bounced around is naturally fun as hell. Terrifying because we could hear the sounds of breaking bones as our tires crushed bodies under them. In more than one case, I saw blood and guts explode out onto the sidewalk as we rolled over an infected gusher. Eventually though, we broke through. The group of infected continued to chase us for about a block before they slowed and eventually stopped, watching us pull away. The rear hummer had become the lead and we followed them further down, trying to put some more distance between us and the attackers.

We eventually pulled to the side of the destroyed road, and it was not by my choice at all. Where the women had decided to pull over was the parking lot of the Route 66 diner. If you know anything about our previous experiences, you'd know that this was by no means a happy place. Rachel, Kenneth and I were extremely agitated, taking up guard duty like we were born for that sole purpose. The kids though couldn't care less where we were and they ran and hugged each other. It would have been absolutely adorable I'm sure had my back not been to them all. This area was in our nightmares, and I just wanted to load up and GTFO (Get the fuck out). The two children that we rescued from the Sub wanted to sit in our Humvee. *Yay*, I thought as I once again took the driver seat before anyone else got in. The rear of our vehicle looked like we had decided to paint the back shades of red and black, it was so absolutely covered with blood. From the rear passenger door all around the rear was just disgusting. I think I might have seen at least two eyes stuck to the left side somehow, and one freaking hand was still grasping onto the gasoline storage bin. I wanted so desperately to start throwing out macabre jokes. I could go into more detail but right then, comedy was not something that I felt like at all. I sat there, peering out of the windshield and saw Kenneth staring across the street and straight at Presbyterian hospital, his gaze unwavering. Isabel came to him and wrapped her arms around him in a tight embrace. Only in an intense drinking session back at the base did Ken finally tell me what had happened that night at the hospital. I knew just how traumatic it had been for him, and the fact that Isabel had broken him into telling her was a testament to her character and to her feelings for him, and his for her. I watched the short exchange in front of my Humvee, and I began to cough, lightly at first, with it quickly turning into a full-blown fit. I felt for several moments as if my lungs were going to rupture out of my mouth. When the coughing was over, I looked down at my hand, which was previously covering my mouth. A splat of blood was centered almost perfectly on it. I stared at the blood, confused. *What the shit?* I asked myself as I just looked at it. The pain from the bite seemed to radiate from my wound to my brain, just in time to remind me just what the fuck was going on. *Oh yeah, I'm dying*, I thought as I continued to stare at the blood. I heard the door to my right open and immediately rubbed the blood against my pant leg. "Are you alright?" Rachel asked me as she got in and sat down. "Yeah, I might be catching a cold," I told her. She glanced over at me, only paying a little bit of attention. "I'm sorry," she said. "Really?!" I asked her, more than a little bit perturbed. I was literally fucking dying and that's all that she had to say? She turned her focus right on me though, and her eyes locked on to mine, and I began to feel that very familiar feeling of my soul hanging above a fire pit that is an angry woman's gaze. "What do you mean, really?" she asked, about ready to lay the smack down on me. It was then that I remembered that I had not told her that I was in fact bitten and a cold in this day and age was the least of our worries. Sharpest tool in the shed. "Sorry hun, I'm just tired," I told her, trying to placate her. Her eyes turned soft in an instant and she reached out a hand to my forehead. "You are a bit warm," she told me with a small hint of worry. "I'll be alright," I told her. She turned her attention as the kids, Cara and Cayden, jumped into the seats in the back. They were obviously thrilled. I wished with all of my being that I could feel that same feeling again someday. Atencio filled in beside the kids. I gave her a questioning glance. "She's going in the other one," she responded, my unspoken question about Ashmore answered. "Alright, let's get the hell out of here," I said. "Language," the young girl from the back seat spoke up. "That's right," Rachel piped in. "Are you guys serious right now?" I asked, as I pulled the vehicle into the center lane to retrace our steps back out of town. "There are children present," Rachel replied. "Well, grab my ears," I responded as we accelerated out of the area.

Chapter Fourteen

What appeared to be the storm to end all storms slammed into us just as we made our way out of Albuquerque. I use the term slammed literally. One moment, we had a light drizzle, the next, we moved into the sheet of rain like a creepy guy into a hot girl's DMs. The wind and the rain shook our Humvee as we drove out of the city. I would have liked to look back and see my once home fade away into the distance, but that was certainly not in the cards. I couldn't see shit out of the mirrors. We drove into the darkness and I felt the tires lose traction more than once. Rachel was hanging on for dear life, her fingernails turning white from where she had her hands bracing herself on the dashboard. As the driver, I had some modicum of control, so for me, it was just another drive in the rain. My passengers, and I'm sure those of the vehicle behind us, had absolutely no control and I'm sure they were screaming inside. I figured we'd burst through the wall of rain any moment and we'd be good to go. There's a saying in New Mexico; if you don't like the weather, cross the street. I've literally done just that, crossing the street and avoiding a nasty bit of hail. I've moved my parked car from one side to the other of a grocery store parking lot just to avoid a bit of rain after a recent car washing. Does this mean that it never rained on my freshly walked truck? Of course not. In fact, I believe washing my vehicle is my version of a white man's rain dance. Almost without fail, less than two days pass before it would rain on my pickup truck. This was not the case this time though, obviously. No rain dance here, just unlucky timing. That or God, the Devil or some other deity had it out for us for some reason. The further that we went, the more intense the storm got. Anyone who has driven in tornado warning weather would know what I'm talking about. That once happened to me during a trip out to Texas. We could hear the sirens in the distance and it was raining hard. I turned to my companion, my now ex fiancé who was visibly frightened by the weather. We could barely see the tail lights of the vehicle in front of us. I had laughed off my nervousness and said, "Look, if there was a tornado nearby, I think it would be hailing." That had seemed to calm her down until wouldn't you know it? It started hailing. Luckily, nothing untoward became of us for that trip but this trip was feeling eerily similar. As we climbed out of the mountain pass following I40 East, I had just a moment to see a shape in front of us as we slammed into it. I heard and saw whatever it was being thrown onto the hood and over the roof of the vehicle as I stepped hard on the brakes, trying desperately to bring the skidding Humvee to an immediate stop. We came to a screeching halt with Kenneth's Humvee coming to a rest right beside mine. I leapt out, nearly slipping on the wet surface of the road and rushed behind our truck. I was horrified as I looked down at a person on the roadway behind us. I hit a person. "Oh shit," I said aloud as I turned the person over. A woman in maybe her mid-twenties was lying before me. I have no doubt she was previously incredibly attractive but her body was damn near destroyed by the impact. Yes, even in the direst of situations, men do, in fact, notice things like that. I didn't see any signs of infection as I used my flashlight to check her. No throat torn out, no limbs missing or any of that crap. Besides the broken bones protruding out of her torn skin in different directions and the obvious road rash, nothing led me to believe that this was anything other than a living breathing person. As I opened her eyelids and saw them lock onto mine, I fell backwards, my ass hitting the ground hard, caught completely off guard. Kenneth had caught up to me and trained his rifle on her. I noted quickly that he was the only other one to have disembarked from the vehicles. Understandable considering the torrent of rain, but not good in a fight. Thankfully, there was only one. The woman on the wet asphalt growled at me as she stared hungrily at me, her tangled body attempting to move towards me. Kenneth didn't hesitate and fired one round into her head. I immediately heard a chorus of moans, seemingly from everywhere around us. The wind again picked up, causing the rain to whip over us and limiting our visibility to mere feet. As lightning flashed through, I spotted the source of the moans. A group of infected was directly in front of the lead Humvee. I had in my haste left the driver side door open. “No!” I shouted as I stood and ran for the opening. An infected had already attempted to climb in as I reached it, its body more than halfway inside. I pulled it backwards and slammed its head into the door jam. I heard a crack and let the limp infected fall to the pavement. The occupants inside had barely registered that it had been an unwelcome guest as the blood from the infected sprayed the driver seat as it was forcibly ejected from the vehicle. I felt hands on me as I leapt for the driver seat, trying to get into the damn truck with the hope of getting it secure. I tried pulling the door closed but several hands were still gripping it, holding it open. It was like the paparazzi trying to get one last shot at some A-list movie star. I changed gears to drive and slammed on the gas, hoping the forward movement would dislodge the icky fingers. The Humvee barreled into a half dozen infected as I tried to accelerate out of the area. A parked car leapt out of the darkness and I swerved to avoid it. Pulling the wheel to the right hard, I saw just a hint of the guard rail as we smashed through it and began tumbling down the bottom of the canyon. Try as I might, I could not regain control of the vehicle as we turned sideways and began barreling down towards a most likely fiery end. Everyone in the vehicle was thrown back and forth, out of the corner of my eye, I saw Rachel become knocked unconscious from her head slamming repeatedly against the window. I wanted to reach out and help her but it was useless. Another roll crushed me against my own window. The children in the back seats were still screaming as the darkness reached out and punched me in the head.

When I finally awoke, I felt cold water on my face and my body was drenched. As I slowly came to consciousness, I began to shake, feeling the incredible cold of the world around me. I moved slowly, feeling part of my body partially submerged in a body of water. I was in an arroyo that had recently seen action. I was most likely some of that action. The concrete under me was not pleasant and I tasted blood in my mouth as I spat it out and began to stand up on shaking legs. My head felt like someone had taken a sledge hammer to it, and I could see a series of bruises forming on nearly every empty inch of visible skin. I could only imagine what my face looked like. For all I knew, I now resembled the hunchback of Notre Dame. When I was finally able to look at my surroundings, I noted there was nothing familiar at all. I had been washed downstream quite a ways by the looks of it. I could still see out of both of my eyes so I had that at least. As I began to come more and more into my own, I realized just how screwed that I was. Have you ever looked around and thought *I'm in danger?* This was my first thought as my mind finally began to catch up with the rest of me. My rifle was missing and the only weapon that I had left intact was a knife still secured to my chest rig. Even my side arm had been ripped away. I pulled the knife out of its metal sheath to confirm that it was in fact intact. The blade glinted in the morning light. *Oh shit, it's morning?* I asked myself as I looked up into the slowly bluing sky. Sure enough, the previous day's storm clouds were moving to the northwest and out of my general area. Movement caught my eye, and I glanced to my right. On one of the banks of the arroyo stood an infected. The skinny dipshit was just staring at me. This would have been creepy as hell had I not been through what I had in the past few days. I returned his stare with my own, not giving any fucks to how ridiculous the entire situation was. The thing took a step forward and fell face first into the concrete-lined arroyo. As it stood back up, its left side of its face had been sheared off almost to the bone from the concrete. It was like a horrific rendition of Gotham City's two face. I about lost what little was in my stomach as I saw its tongue hanging out from where its cheek used to be. After my gag reflex finally settled down and after the zombie had made it about half of the distance in my direction, I began my trek towards it. I had no idea where I was, where my crew was, how the hell I even got to this spot as the last thing that I had remembered was sitting inside of a Humvee. Yet, now this asshole wants to try to make a meal out of me? Not today, Satan. I swung my knife-wielding right arm and the pointy end went straight through the soft spot in the skull and through its temple. It stood there, with its eyes rolling back into its head as I pulled the weapon out with a plop. It dropped and proceeded to spill what was left of its diseased brain onto the concrete at my feet.

The blackened brain pieces wiggled and jiggled as they spread out onto the concrete as if they were made by Jell-O. That did it as I blew chunks as I tried to pull my eyes from the event.

I assumed that I was downstream from where I had not so gently left the Hummer. If only because it felt like I was on a never-ending hill with the ground literally feeling tilted. I didn't see any other wreckage at all, no evidence to show how I had been deposited here. The only thing that I could think of to do was to begin my walk back up towards the top. Hopefully, I would find the crew and we could get back to base and everything would be dandy. My optimism made a teeny tiny appearance for just a few steps then quickly dissipated as I walked, and walked and yeah, walked some more. After what felt like an eternity, I finally began to see bits and pieces of metal along the arroyo. It was just a hint of a piece there, an ammo box here. The damage to my body was making every step forward excruciating. Each step seemed to cause pain to radiate from head to toe. As they say though, momma didn't raise a quitter and I trucked along. As I looked up, trying to cover my eyes partly from the sun, I saw it, a large pile of debris. I rushed up another quarter of a mile and spotted the husk of the Humvee. It was damn near a crushed tuna can. A sick feeling gripped my gut with the force of a hulk-sized fist punching me, and I ran for it, or I suppose it would have been much closer to a limp had anyone been watching. Feeling despair fill my heart as I reached the vehicle, I peered in, expecting to see bodies and blood and everything you'd imagine of a destructive car wreck. There was indeed blood but no bodies. *Oh no,* I thought as I stared at the empty seats. Were my friends and those little kids now zombies, wondering the desert? Were they out there somewhere after suffering some horrible death because of me? I hit my knees, feeling the pain rush through me. Yeah, I'll admit it. I cried like a baby. The feeling of failure, the pain of loss, and the all-encompassing feeling of loneliness rushed through me as I sobbed. The sobbing soon turned to anger as I placed my forehead to the dirt. I punched the sand around me as if that would somehow fix anything. Several minutes passed and I laid flat against the Earth, wishing for death to come and end all of these feelings of emptiness. My tear-laced right eye spotted something unusual. A voice in my head told me to shut the hell up, I did just that. Isn't that a symptom of insanity? To have voices in your head? Or isn't that just a sign of the human condition and something that we all have that most just ignore? I saw footprints in the dried mud. My inner feelings of overall feeling shitty came to an abrupt halt as I slowly stood back up, fixing my stare at the prints. Two larger sets of prints and two smaller sets. Granted, the larger sets weren't much larger than the smaller two by much, but it was enough to be noticeable. *They were okay*, I thought as my eyes traced the path of the tracks as they appeared to head away from the crash. They had to be okay to walk away from that crash. That voice in my head shut that down with a *Or they were all zombies when they walked away?* I began to walk in the same direction as the tracks. In front of me and up a bit of a climb was the bent and destroyed guard rail. This was it, I thought as I rushed forward, keeping the foot prints ever in my view. I climbed and made it to the top to see…. Nothing. Okay, well, not nothing. Bodies littered the road, and spent bullet casings were everywhere. Tire tracks were left in blood which stopped parallel to the broken rail. The footprints in the dirt ended right at the start of the old asphalt. Burnt rubber marks were evident as whatever vehicle had been there had taken off with great haste back down the mountain pass, back to Albuquerque. I was alone. *Maybe it was for the best?* I thought as I put one foot in front of the other and began to walk again, following the pavement back down the pass. My goal was to make it back to the city to see if I could somehow signal my companions. Weaponless and with no ride, it would be a hell of a trip. Like the soldier that I tried to be, I shrugged, and walked forward on the long road ahead.

Once again, I was by myself, I thought as I put one foot in front of the other and continued my trek. *Just fricken dandy.* As I trucked along, with only my mind to keep me company which probably was not healthy at all. When you are bored with the only entertainment a small rock that you're kicking back and forth on a broken and uneven roadway, your mind tends to go all over the damn place. As the rock once again got stuck in a crevice, I bent down to unwedge it and I stopped. My ears perked up as if that was possible, and I heard a sound that I was all too familiar with. It was the sound of a helicopter. *Holy fuck, I'm saved,* I thought. I waved my arms, not even seeing the chopper yet. Like an angel riding the clouds, a jet black painted UH-60 black hawk rode over the mountain and into clear view. It apparently spotted me, as it rocked back and forth and then flew past, hopefully, to turn back around and head back to me. *Finally, something went right!* I thought as I fist pumped the air. It was then that a wave of nausea came over me. I gagged, throwing up nothing but saliva. My stomach cramped and my hand went to my midsection. It didn't stop, if anything, it got worse. I felt a wave of heat radiate through my body, and sweat began to pour off of me in the roadway. I hit the ground hard, my hands instinctively staying at my gut, not helping at all. It was worse than any kind of pain I had previously felt. My heart continued to pound hard in my chest, and the impulse to throw up would not leave me. I screamed, letting the whole world in on my agony. The sound of the helicopter's rotors were nearing as the pain washed over me like a tidal wave. With one last scream of pain, I passed out in the middle of Route 66.

Chapter Fifteen: Several hours earlier

Rachel hung on for everything that she was worth as the vehicle rolled end over end. As her head smacked against her window for the third time, darkness enveloped her as she lost consciousness. When she awoke, the window to her right had shattered and was now at ground level. She spat the taste of blood and dirt from her mouth as she tried to move. Her straps had held but she felt her entire body bruised and beaten. She stirred slowly, trying to look around as she did so. The Humvee was on one side, her side. "Shep?" she whispered as she was finally able to look over at the driver side that was now the top of the enclosure. She did a double take. Shepherd was gone. Rachel felt panic begin to well up inside of her as she struggled to move out of her straps. Finally, she was able to disengage them and fell against the door.

She worked at it for several minutes, righting herself. Finally, she was able to stand inside the vehicle and looked into the rear seats. The children and Atencio were still there, but unmoving. She shimmied her body into the rear seats and one by one, checked their vitals. They were miraculously still alive. She slowly shook each one and realized that the rain from the storm was pouring in from the open door up top. A large pool was forming at the now bottom of the cab. It wouldn't flood the vehicle for a while but they couldn't just sit and wait for it to happen either. As they each groggily awoke from their sleepy times, the children began to panic. The pain that they were all feeling would no doubt be a shock to their systems. They screamed and they cried, she tried her best to comfort them. It didn't work very well though. Frightened children, or even happy children are the hardest type of people to try to calm down. Rachel had moved onto Atencio who was not waking up. She shook her several times, and again felt for a pulse. It was present although a bit weak. A bleeding head wound on the right side of her skull came into view. The pop pop pop of what sounded like gunfire caught Rachel's attention. She glanced up at the driver door aka the roof and spotted something blocking the view of the clouds above. An infected was crawling into the opening. It fell in hard, causing the children to, once again, begin to scream. Rachel took action, looking everywhere for a weapon but coming up empty. She kicked at the zombie who was trying to right itself and pull itself into the backseat of the Humvee. The infected reached out on kick seven and grabbed a hold of her boot. The action took Rachel off guard and she slipped, falling down on the slippery interior. The creature, what had previously been an old man wearing khakis, a button up shirt and a tie, then had her with both hands and as much as she struggled, it would not let go. The strength of the undead man was incredible. It proceeded to pull her towards its mouth, greedily eying its prey, and it was winning the battle. A deafening shot rang out in the tiny confines of the truck. Rachel felt the undead lose its grip and let go, causing her to fall backwards and onto the kids. She could not hear anything other than a loud constant ringing in her ears, but she saw the smoke from a pistol being held up by Atencio. Her right eye had begun to swell up but that had obviously not hindered her from taking the shot.

Rachel stood back up and helped the children out of their buckles. The rain seemed to get worse much to their chagrin. They were soaked by the rain pouring in from the open windows up top. The sound of gunfire had picked up its pace and she recognized the only thing that it could be. Her friends on the road trying to take down the crowd of infected. If there were too many of those evil things, their team would be forced to leave them behind if they had to. Staying in the car overnight in the rain was a no go for her and everyone else with her. "We have to move," she told the other occupants of the Humvee as she helped Atencio stand. She was definitely worse for wear but she didn't quit. The woman was a fighter. They all climbed from the destroyed vehicle. From the pouring rain and into the pouring rain, only now they did not have the limited protection of the doors or the vehicle interior. As Rachel hit the ground, she looked around for Shepherd. It was dark, but using the flashing of the lighting above to her advantage, her eyes strained to glimpse anything. There was no sign of him at all. No footprints in the mud, none of his gear. It was as if he had just disappeared. The whimpering of the two children did not allow her to ponder on it for long. She took the lead as they all began to walk up the mountainside to the broken guard rail. The sound of automatic gunfire was still present, and it helped to usher them faster and faster. There was no telling when the group on the road would drive off and leave them for dead. Atencio helped to keep the kids on track, urging them along. Even battered and bruised, the children moved forward, without a single vocal complaint. As they neared the edge of the guardrail, Rachel heard shouting. "They're over here!" It was Jaylin. Her rifle was at the ready and her flashlight shone brightly over the broken railing. It was as if it were the light guiding them to Heaven. Rachel took Jaylin's hand and with a strong pull, Rachel was roadside. A group of infected was situated in the lights of the 2nd Humvee with Kenneth, and Ashmore laying down a wall of lead. Jaylin spotted one making a go for the newly found group and drilled it through the right eye, dropping it like a rock. "Let's go!"

she yelled to the group below. They all did what they were told and urgently made their way up to the road and headed for the vehicle. Atencio, naturally was taking up the rear defense, and firing shots from her pistol into the horde as they did. Rachel pulled the rear passenger door open and the kids jumped in, still completely distraught. Kenneth was falling back, his rifle smoking with each round leaving the chamber. "There's too many, we've got to go now!" he shouted to Jaylin. He glanced over and saw the women and children enter the vehicle and looked back at Jaylin. "Shepherd?" His one-word question was met with a slow shake of Jaylin's head. His eyes fell from hers, and he turned and fired the rest of his magazine into the crowd before them, his anger evident. Jaylin opened the passenger door, jumping in and closing it behind her. He made it in just as the horde made it to the vehicle. "God damned zombies!" he said in frustration as he started the vehicle and began to reverse back the way they came. As soon as he had room, he made a U-turn and headed back into Albuquerque. "We're going back?" Atencio asked. "We've got to find a way through that big ass group of infected. We might have to wait it out a bit," he said. "Well, that's just great," Atencio blurted out. "What the fuck do you want me to do about it?" he asked, glancing at her through the rear view. "Nothing, I was just saying," she replied, a bit abashed. "We've got no other choice. We're going back," he said matter of factly as they barreled back towards Albuquerque.

Chapter Sixteen

Several hours later or so I guessed, I awoke in a hospital bed. This was strange enough as the last thing that I saw was the asphalt coming straight up to my face. My eyes traced around the room as I took it all in. I was not a stranger to hospital rooms, as I tended to be accident-prone in my previous life. As I looked around at the equipment, I noticed that they were all in pristine condition. *These were new*, I thought as I looked from wall to wall. The equipment at base, while kept clean were not this nice. Especially after the last zombie attack on the base, all of the equipment got some serious use. The lighting was not bright but not dull either. Just enough to do the job without burning my skin off. Directly in front of me was a fairly large mirror, as if for some strange ass reason, I wanted to look at myself dying. *Who the hell designs these rooms anyway?* I questioned myself as I stared at myself in the reflection. Even with the dirt cleaned off, I was still bruised in more than one place. I felt sorer than I had ever been, as if I had run a back to back marathon while lifting weights. *Oh shit, the bite.* The thought popped into my head and I looked down to see the wound on my arm with a clean bandage around it. I had thought for sure that if a bite was found, I'd just be shot. *This is interesting*, I thought as I lay back down, wondering what the absolute hell. If they saw the bite and knew what it was, I'd be dead in a heartbeat, so what in the hell and Satan's girl scout cookies was going on here? It was then that a woman entered the room, as if on cue. Her face was mostly covered by a medical mask and she was wearing scrubs. Nothing besides her skin tone and her fiery blue eyes were visible. "How are you feeling?" she asked as she stood beside my bed. "I'm feeling fine, besides feeling like I went ten rounds with a professional boxer with my hands tied behind my back." "Good. Good," she stated, looking over the readings on the equipment around me. *Wow, what a sense of humor.* "Where the hell am I?" I asked her, staring straight into her eyes. "You're safe now. You're in the medical wing of a government facility known as DUCC NM." I stared at her blankly. She chuckled quietly, apparently amused. "Deep Underground Command Center NM. I'm guessing you know what the NM stands for?" I nodded with a roll of my eyes. "We are just one of many former government installations build around the country to ensure the continuation of the US in the event of a catastrophe. This compound was just a lot of fancy military tech being tested outside of prying eyes. One of these bunkers was built in every state in the union." I nodded. "I can understand that, I guess. Uncle Sam always has a plan B," I said as I stared at her as she apparently took some notes on my chart. "Anyway, just relax and we will have you on your feet in no time. It looks like you were severely dehydrated, and you were pretty beaten up when we found you. What were you doing in the middle of nowhere in an apocalypse?" she asked, her eyes seeming to dig into me. "I was being chased by a bunch of those things. I didn't exactly have a way out," I told her. "Besides, it was a beautiful day for a stroll," I said. She just nodded; her apparent humor gone. "Alright. What's your name?" she asked. "Barnes," I told her, giving up on cracking jokes. Some people just don't mesh well with me. She raised an eyebrow. "Just Barnes?" she asked. "Yeah, there's really no need for two names these days, is there?" I asked in return. "No, I suppose not. Alright, Mr. Barnes, you'll stay here and continue to get healthy. In the meantime, I'll report to my superiors about you being in relatively good health. They need good people to help support their cause," she said as she turned to leave. "And what cause is that, exactly?" I asked. "To unite the world under one government," she said as she patted my knee. "What's your name?" I asked her just as she was leaving the room. She stopped and turned back to me. "Sydney," she replied as she continued out the door and into the hallway. *Sydney*, I repeated to myself as I lay back down into the not-really-comfortable-at-all bed. To unite the world under one government. *That sounded shady as hell*, I thought as I once again passed back into unconsciousness, the pain from my battered and bruised body flaring up and encouraging me to go night night.

On the other side of the mirror, a man stood staring at the new patient before him. A door in the room opened and a nurse entered. The man slowly turned, nodding to her as he did so, keeping the new guest in his periphery. "How is our new friend doing?" The man, in full military uniform stood perfectly erect, his eyes staring directly at the nurse into what she felt like was her soul. "He's fine medically," she said, coming to stand beside the man. "General, it's very unorthodox to let someone with a bite be unrestrained," she said quietly. "Yes, it is. Desperate times call for desperate measures though, don't they?" he asked. "Yes Sir," she replied. "Besides, I'd like to see if he would be more cooperative than the others. This man and the others like him are the key for us. We just have to figure out how to wield our new weapons," he said, a grin creeping onto his face. A shudder fell over the nurse. "What about the zombies in this wing?" "Every experiment needs a control, don't you think?" he replied. "If anything happens…" she began to say. He cut her off quickly, "This is the most secure base short of Mt. Weather and NORAD. My soldiers have this handled," he said, his tone leaving no room for argument. "Yes sir," she said back, a bit mechanically. "Good girl," he said, patting her lightly on the shoulder as he moved to walk past her. "The Praetor will see soon enough. The whole world will." His hand left her, and he grabbed the door handle and walked out, the metal door coming to a close with a soft click. Sydney stood watching the man in the room before her sleep. He was one of five bitten but not turned people that they've found since everything went to hell. He was the first one that they've left unrestrained. There were also thirty infected in different stages being monitored in rooms just like this one. If General Hawkings wanted a weapon, odds are he'd find a way to make one here. *God help us if he makes the virus go airborne*, she thought, feeling another shudder of ice cold roll up her back. Her watch beeped and she sighed. Time to make the rounds with the others. She placed the mask back on her face as she too left the room.

Down the hall from Shepherd's room stood the first row of zombie-occupied monitoring rooms. A lone infected stared into the one-way mirror, as if admiring itself for some extended period of time. As the technician on the other side left the hidden room, the infected moved to the door to its room, spending several minutes staring at the keycard reader and door handle. Two minutes later, the keycard reader turned green and the door opened with several men in full riot gear entering, followed by the technician. The infected lunged, and was rewarded with a plastic shield strike to the face, causing it to be pushed backwards, further into the room. The protected soldiers pushed the infected back until it was in the far corner of the room, as away from the door. Behind them, the tech opened the top of a cage containing several white mice and spilled the contents out. Four large mice scurried about the unused hospital bed. The tech then left the room, and the protected troops retreated, keeping the zombie in their sights. By that time though, there was no need. The mice had caught the eye of the undead and it chased and grabbed them each one by one. It fed, feeling the warm blood seep into its mouth as it bit deeply. Broken teeth tore into the flesh of the small helpless creatures, blood spraying in a small arc onto the wall closest to it. As the men filed out of the room, the infected watched the soldiers depart the room. It had been watching as the tech had scanned his key card to unlock the door on his way out. The dawn of recognition was slow to ignite in its cold mind, but eventually it did. It fed almost gleefully knowing that soon, it would not be dining on these little vermin but would soon be feasting on the humans that had just left. Soon.

Chapter Seventeen

Back in Albuquerque, those remaining survivors of the Cannon AFB group sat huddled around a small fireplace. After returning from losing one of their own, Kenneth had found a secluded house in the northeast heights to rest up. After unloading all of the occupants, and clearing the house, room by room, they then retrieved whatever they could of value. From canned corn to firewood, it was all gathered in the home's living room. Although they were able to change out some of their clothing, the icy feeling of cold from the rain had been felt down to their bones. In hopes of fixing that, Rachel had ordered a fire made. Kenneth disagreed, saying that it would draw attention. It was the children though that Rachel was concerned about. They were still shaking from the cold and they did not make this trip out here just to lose the four kids to pneumonia. Eventually, Ken relented, and the fire was made. Slowly, everyone inched closer and closer to the fireplace until they were just a big blob of humanity, trying to get every bit of warmth that they could. After what felt like hours, everyone had fallen asleep, with the heat continuing to hug them in its warm embrace. While everyone slept, Joe and Raul had made their way out of the pile of people and slowly made their way out of the house. Joe, the older of the two children, led his younger brother quietly out of the back door and into the cold of the night. These adults almost killed them all and they were safer on their own, he had told his brother. The other children, Cara and Cayden did not feel the same way and they wanted no part in leaving. *That was fine,* thought Joe, *two less other kids to worry about.* As he led his younger brother from house to house, he walked into an open parcel of land with a large 'for sale' sign still hung up on the side facing the main road. They walked in the pitch dark, the remnants of the storm not far off in the distance. A quick flash of lighting silhouetted the horde from earlier that day. They were less than a mile away on the main road; Tramway. *Uh oh*, he thought as he grabbed his brother's hand and tried to move them along in another direction. As they trudged through the dirt lot in that direction, he could hear glass breaking and the moans of several infected from just across the street. They, once again, halted in their tracks. The younger of the two children began to cry, with Joe feeling lost. He turned to his left to head back in the direction of the house that they had come. His brother's hand clenched tightly in his as they began to walk back and a lone figure stood directly in their path. It had appeared almost as if from nowhere. The lone figure stood up straight and tall as the rain once again began to fall. Whatever it was did not move an inch as it stood like a statue before them. Joe spoke up. "Hello?" he asked the figure, trying not to shake with fear as he did. He could hear the moans of the infected as if they were all around them, seeming to get closer with each moment. The children had to leave; Joe knew, but this man was in their way. Was he here to help? "Can you help us?" the child asked. The figure shook its head from side to side and took a slow step forward. The two children took two small steps back, recoiling. The moans around them now seemed to be at a crescendo. "They're everywhere!" Raul yelled out while his tears flowed like the rain continuing to fall around the two boys. Joe once again took the little boy's hand and tried to make it past the figure in front of them. With amazing speed, Joe was pulled into the air and with unnatural force, was thrown back into the dirt field. He landed with a loud thump and an audible crack of his left leg. The field was now completely surrounded by infected that were slowly but steadily making their way towards the small food before them. The younger boy stood stock-still and cried, having just watched his older brother tossed like he was a rag doll. The figure walked to and then stood next to the young boy and placed its large hand on the boy's shoulder as if to comfort him. The boy could not move, the fear enveloping every fiber of his small being. He was then unceremoniously picked up under his armpits and raised until he was face to face with the figure. The figure resembled that of a middle-aged man and even now, seemed like one. His short black hair, dark brown eyes and creases from years of happy retirement. To the young boy though, he was scary. Far scarier than the zombies approaching around them. The man smiled, and opened his mouth wide, broken teeth shone brightly with the illumination of a quick flash of lightning. He sank his teeth deep into the young boy's throat, the child's screams cutting off almost immediately. The figure held the child with its strong arms and bit into him, enjoying every moment of the warm blood pouring from the boy who thankfully fell into unconsciousness. The wound was not a traditional feeding by any means and as it felt the boy's life drain away, the monster unceremoniously dropped the child into the dirt and watched in fascination as the older boy attempted to run away, with the rest of the undead zombies in close pursuit. With a broken leg, he would not get far. Watching the small prey struggle only made him hungrier, but he knew he had plans and would wait for this human child at his feet to turn. Then step two of his plan would be ready. He grinned as the older boy dodged an outstretched arm, then another, but was hit from the side by a previously unseen infected. The boy gasped; the air being completely emptied from his lungs. A zombie took a bite out of one of his arms, and the boy screamed, only to be pounced on by two more undead. With relative ease, they took him to the ground and began to ravish the young body under them. The long figure stood watching, knowing there would not be much left to turn. More and more zombies showed up to dinner and pushed and shoved to get whatever pieces of the now dead boy. By his feet, the younger boy began to stir. *Good*, the figure thought. *Time to get the rest of the humans out of that house and into my stomach.*

Two streets down, the sound of Joe's screaming woke Jaylin up. She stood and stretched, attempting to wipe away the exhaustion from her eyes. She did a quick headcount, her eyes moving over each bundled up person around her. Coming up two people short, she immediately took action. "Everyone up!" she yelled out. Everyone began to stir but not enough to her liking. "Raul and Joe are missing. Everyone get your asses up!" she yelled, emphasizing her point with a kick to Ken's ass. The women in the group were up in record time and began to search the house. Kenneth, who was still fighting off sleep from exhaustion was the last to rise. As he finally stood, out of habit, he grabbed his rifle, which had been leaning next to him against the wall as he had slept. As his fingers wrapped around the weapon, the front door to the house opened slowly. Cara and Cayden were now fully awake and looked at the open door with Ken. The silhouette of a young boy was visible in the now stormy exterior. Kenneth sighed. "Ladies, I found them, they're fine," he said, still groggy, he stood and made his way to the door. "You two really shouldn't be outside right now…" His sentence cut off as the young boy leapt for him, completely knocking him on his ass. "What the fuck?!" Ken yelled as he tried desperately to get the crazy kid off of him. The child's mouth was snapping, trying to seek purchase anywhere on Ken's body. The kid's eyes were pitch black, the previously soft whites around his pupils were bloodshot, and hostility oozed from the child. The thought of infection instantly spread through Kenneth's mind. His mindset clicked from *is the kid alright* to *I need to kill this kid* in just a couple of his heartbeats. He went from being on the defense to offense, like his mind had flipped a switch. He pushed the kid off of him, and using his own long legs to gain momentum. He slammed the small child up against the wall by the door. He couldn't bring his rifle to bare, so he grabbed his knife from his pocket, flicking it open with the touch of a button. In pre-zombapoc times, switch blades were illegal in New Mexico. Now, who gave a shit? He stabbed upwards, feeling the sharp blade move its way from the kid's chin into his brain. The longer than normal blade did the job and the child stopped flailing about. A noise caught his attention and Ken turned to see Infected that were flooding into the house from the open door. He turned back to see the child's face. The child, Joe, his eyes now closed, and completely slack against Ken's arms. "I'm sorry, Joe," Kenneth whispered as he dropped the now lifeless body of the child and bolted to the side, attempting to slam the front door closed. There was a half dozen infected already in, but he was now trying to stem the tide. The door caught on the foot of an infected and he repeatedly slammed the door against it, hearing the foot break but still not getting it closed. "A little fucking help down here would be fucking dandy!" he yelled to the other members of his group. He could hear the sound of footsteps on the floor above him as they finally heard him and were heading back down to assist. The two kids, Cara and Cayden though were holding it down in the meantime. As Ken watched with his back against the wooden door, two of the six remaining infected went down as they were both speared through their eyes. *Ninja kids*, Ken thought as finally, reinforcements arrived. Isabel took two steps between the next infected and the children and drilled it through the head with a well-aimed shot. The other women filed into the room and finished the others off with no problem. Around them, they heard the shattering of glass as more zombies entered from every available entry point. *All we wanted was a little bit of rest, but no, now we have to entertain a shit ton of guests*, Kenneth thought as he finally made some progress with getting the door closed. All he had to do was kick a now severed foot back outside to get the door shut. This macabre version of footsies was creepy to say the least, but it had to be done. As his boot sent the foot spinning out into the darkness, he locked the deadbolt and swung back around, his rifle now up and ready, he took in the room around him. Dozens of zombies were breaking in. They fell through the windows and began to enter through the now destroyed back door. *The back door is always the weak point,* Ken thought as he continued his quick observation. Gunshots were going off all around him and Cara was trying hard to get into the fight with her homemade spear. Time seemed to slow down as he looked from side to side. Rachel and Isabel were in the kitchen, firing into the mass of infected reaching in through that window. Jaylin and Atencio were at the back of the house, almost out of his line of sight, trying to not so gently push them back out the backdoor. Cara and Cayden were back to back, covering each other's flanks as they watched for any new targets in the main living room. Sheer numbers would win this game and Ken knew it. As time once again sped up, he shouted. "Everyone upstairs!" It was the only thing that he could think of. It was far easier to defend one staircase than it was to try to with all of these windows and doors. *Play smarter, not harder. I wish I had some damn cheat codes*, he thought as he pointed at Cara and Cayden then pointed to the stairs, urging them to get moving forward. The children were first up, bounding up the stairs quickly. Ashmore had been upstairs, raining lead from above into the horde below. She now was at the top of the stairs, ushering everyone else up. Rachel was next, followed by Isabel and Jaylin. Atencio took up the rear, still battered and bruised from the car ride earlier. The zombies flooded into the house and made a beeline for the stairs. If their lives had not been on the line, it might have been fairly comical to see so many shuffling zombies push and cajole each other out of the way, attempting to give chase at a speed that a doped-up snail could outrun. Kenneth was pushed back as something hit the front door that he was still up against. The force of the impact sent him sprawling and into the arms of one of the snail runners. This one was a dumb dumb who seemed to at first, not even notice as it began to hug Kenneth with open arms. "Sorry, I'm not ready for a committed relationship," Ken said as he ducted under the zombie and pushed it out of the way. The front door burst open, the hinges clattering to the floor in the living room. The lone figure stood in the doorway, looking at the events playing out before it. Kenneth made it to the stairs at the same time as the front walking zombies. The women upstairs were picking their targets well and fired off round after round, keeping a lane open for Ken. He tripped two infected and finally reached the steps, jumping up them three at a time. When he reached the top, he was slammed against one side of the walls as a dresser made its way tumbling towards the bottom of the steps. It squished, for a lack of a better word, one unlucky zombie at the bottom. "Poor guy was underdressed," Ken blurted out with a grin. All of the guns stopped firing as the women stopped to peer over at him. "It's because he re-died by a clothes' dresser. Get it?" he asked, smiling broadly. The women just looked at each other, each one shaking their heads and resumed their work. Other pieces of furniture soon found their way to the bottom of the steps, minus the jokes. The infected had to climb over each piece as if it was a new game show for a million dollars. Someone fired a round at the figure still by the front door but it missed its mark, hitting the wall slightly to its left. It ducked, and moved into the kitchen directly to its right. *It ducked* thought Ken as it watched the scene unfold. It must be one of the smart infected. That was the only conclusion that he could make at this point in time. Bodies began to pile up along with the furniture below creating a wonderful corpse-filled barricade. Eventually, the entirety of the steps was packed with bodies and it effectively sealed off the downstairs. As the last round left the chamber, they all stood, still panting from the exertion and the adrenaline pumping through them that it took several minutes for them to calm down enough to stop reacting and start thinking.

"What the actual fuck?" Rachel asked the group, still trying to take in much needed oxygen. "It was a trap," Kenneth said as he slowly reloaded magazine after magazine, still keeping an eye on the pile at the stairs. "A trap?" she asked. "Yes. They waited until someone separated from the group, then they surrounded us." "Who separated?" Jaylin asked. "The two boys. They're dead," Ken said, somewhat robotically. "What do you mean they're dead?" Rachel said, pushing Ken up against the wall. His eyes immediately cut daggers at her as he rebounded from the drywall. "I mean I literally killed the one that attacked me, and based on the amount of fresh blood on the zombies that entered the house in the initial rush, they didn't stop with the one kid. That's what the fuck I mean," he said, staring the woman down. Her eyes though showed that the anger that had been welling within her was gone, and erased by sorrow. Tears began to streak down her face and she sat on the steps and began to cry. The other women all gathered around and shared in her grief. They could fill a small sink with the amount of tears pouring from the group. Ken, on the other hand, watched the pile intently and continued to reload with whatever ammunition that he could find. He had managed to save his own backpack and most of the group had theirs but not the two extra duffle bags that were unaccounted for. The loss hit Ken hard as those had held a majority of the extra ammo. The pile below shifted, slowly at first. It caught his eye and he stared at the dead zombie in the top right of the pile in the stairs. He watched as the dead undead was pulled from the pile, leaving a small gap. The next one was pulled back and the next. A hole was forming quickly. "Ladies, I hate to sound like an asshole right now but get your shit together. We're about to start round two," he said, pulling the rifle up to his shoulder. He heard the group start to breakup and safeties clicking off. Grief or not, survival came first for these women. He watched as an infected's face popped up into the newly made path and he rewarded it with a round to its nose. It was disgusting to see results of a 5.56 round at close range going through the front of its face, and exit out the back. It fell forward but that infected was also yanked back as another body from the pile was pulled out, causing a small avalanche of bodies. In the room beyond, filling the room to capacity stood dozens of zombies, all hungrily staring at them. Ken felt a bit naked as they all looked at him as if he were the last piece of pizza at a stoner's get together after an hour of dabs.

"Everyone, slowly move upstairs. Find a room that has a strong door and a large window," Ken whispered. The remaining children were already upstairs, and one by one, the women backed up slowly and moved up the stairs. Finally, it was just Kenneth alone on the stairs. Behind the set of closest zombies, he could see the figure from before. It was grinning at him. "Wipe that smug ass look off of your ugly face," Kenneth said, raising his rifle. With a wave of the figure's hand, the closest group made a go for

Ken. Pulling his rifle around to the new threat, his round missed the figure and went wide. The infected were now almost over the pile. Four of them were bounding towards him. Behind them, another wave was right behind. He fired two more shots and leapt up the stairs two at a time. The difference between a zombie and an infected was that a zombie was for all intents and purposes, just a walking corpse. A walking dead. The infected, on the other hand, were still for all intents and purposes, living. They were fast, intelligent and had much more dexterity. However, instead of a person with a cold, they had the Z-bug and their entire purpose was to spread it to others, while enjoying a snack. It made those abominations much more dangerous. No one had any idea about the side effects of the infection. It was believed that any sense of their wellbeing or even their soul was burned out during the turning phase, when the infection caused a massive spike in temperature. It was not long after that they tended to get up and start running after the next tasty morsel. At the end of the hall, as he guessed was a master bedroom, the door was open and Isabel was waving him forward, as if he needed extra incentive. The other women were on their knees, with rifles aiming his way. "Please don't miss, please don't miss," he whispered to himself as he ran. One of the infected had nearly caught up and received a bullet to the neck as it tried to take a swipe at Ken. Another was taken down as it rounded the corner from the stairs immediately after. The hall began filling with smoke as Ken made it to the door. He looked back as a half dozen or so had made it nearly all of the way to their door. He slammed it closed, and locked it. A bookcase in the room was pushed in front of the door to help secure it. The large open window already had the screen removed and Rachel was peering down. "It looks clear," she said. Kenneth fired four shots through the door and into the group on the other side. Rachel turned to look at him, questioning his action. "We want to keep them occupied while we make our escape. We don't want them looking for another way in," he said as he too looked down from the window. There was an old station wagon parked under the window. *That was mighty convenient*, Ken thought as the plan formed in his head. "Alright. Rachel, you go first. Aim for the car. Once you hit the ground, secure the area. The kids will go down next. If you start to get overrun, make a go for the vehicles and come back for us. She glanced at him. "We'll be fine. Just do it," he said. She reluctantly nodded. Using a series of bed sheets tied together, Rachel was lowered down onto the car hood below. As soon her feet touched the metal, her rifle was up and the sheet rope was raised back up. "Where the hell did you learn how to tie knots like these?" Atencio asked, watching him pull the rope up. "Boy Scouts," he replied. She stared at him. "Are you serious?" she asked. He stopped long enough to stare at her. "Eagle Scout at your service," he said as he resumed his pulling. She shrugged and grabbed a hold to pull the end up. The kids were prepped and were sent down next, one by one. Atencio had placed six more rounds into the door to keep the undead in their feeding frenzy. As Jaylin was lowered down next, the bedroom door began to bulge inwards. "We should probably hurry this up," Ashmore said. "Ya think?" Atencio replied. "Ladies, focus on the real enemy please," Ken said, as he continued to lower Jaylin down. A moment later, she was safely down, and he was bringing up the sheets for the next person. That left Isabel, himself, Atencio and

Ashmore. In retrospect, he realized that if he was the last one down, there would be no one to lower him down. *Whoops, poor planning on my part,* he thought as he began to lower Isabel. The bedroom door splintered, and shards flew across the room. The remaining two women opened fire, further peppering the door with bullet holes. Thumps of bodies hitting the floor on the other side could be heard. Ken tried to ignore it, his sole mission right then was to get as many people down as possible. Isabel was holding onto the sheet for dear life as Ken looked into her eyes as he kissed her lovingly before lowering her down into the darkness. As Isabel hit the hood of the car, gunfire erupted outside. "Shit shit shit!" Ken said aloud as he lifted the sheets back up as quickly as he could. Sure enough, the infected were now converging on the group outside. He looked out the window and saw the zombies and infected piling out of the house and towards the waiting team. "Go!" Ken yelled. Atencio and Ashmore stood beside him, watching the same spectacle. "Get in the truck and get out of here! Now!" he shouted. Rachel was looking straight at him from the driver window of the Humvee. The writing was on the wall. Everyone piled in. As the horde closed the distance, slamming into the side of the vehicle, it started up and pulled down the driveway back towards Tramway Boulevard, leaving the three remaining members behind. Jaylin watched from the rear window, seeing the three of them silhouetted in the window as they took a left turn and left the house and their friends behind.

Chapter Eighteen

Several hundred miles away, I woke up. Again. I was fairly impressed with that, as I had still expected to either be shot or turned by now. The fact that I was neither surprised the hell out of me. The nurse, Sydney, woke me up while checking my vitals again. I felt worlds better and told her so. She smiled, and I smiled back. "Do you have a minute?" I asked her. Her eyebrow lifted as if her face was asking the obvious question of why. "I'd just like to talk for a bit if you have time." Her face lightened and she glanced down at her watch. Apparently, content with what she saw, she sat on the bed, her scrubs bunching up as she did. Her breasts were pushed firmly against the fabric and it took an epic amount of self-control to not stare at those fine teeter totters. Instead, like the gentleman that I was, I focused on her eyes. They were stunning, with a hint of shyness in them. It was not hard for us to hit it off. Our conversations drifted from our previous lives pre-zombapoc, to our favorite foods and what we missed the most since the world kicked the bucket. A country girl, she had moved across the country to get away from a checkered past with bad habits. She started fresh in New Mexico and it had been the best decision that she had ever made. Living in a small house outside of Santa Fe when it all went down; she had worked at a local clinic when everything went to shit. The fact that she had gotten out was a testament to her strength. It was actually quite refreshing to have a conversation with a decent person without zombies trying to get into the building. I let my guard down in more ways than one. I felt safe for the first time in what seemed like forever. I didn't really feel free, as I was in a hospital room with an IV and a series of other gadgets hooked up to me, but I felt safe. Secure. She left the room after a hefty amount of time, and I wished her goodbye. As she left, I turned to my side and drifted off into a truly restful sleep.

When I awoke next, the room was dark, and if I had to guess, I would say it was early AM. I shifted in my hospital bed, and glanced about the room. Nothing was out of the ordinary. As I closed my eyes though, my mind replayed what I saw and I opened them again. I looked back at the large mirror in the room. There was ambient light coming from the other side. *What in the actual fuck*, I thought as I scrutinized it further. As I squinted hard, I could see something. The outline of a person on the other side. Instantly, I realized it. This was no normal hospital room, it was an observation room, and some fucker was watching me. That, more than anything got my blood boiling. I am sure as shit not cute when I sleep. Truth be told, Rachel on more than one occasion, had just simply pushed me off of the cot back at base because I was either snoring or drooling or making some unexplainable facial expression in my sleep. After the third time of waking up on the hard floor, I realized how the hell I had made it to the ground. She found a way to more than make it up to me. *Holy hell did I miss my Rachel*, I thought as my thoughts though quickly went away from that happy memory train and back to my original tracks. Someone was watching me snore and drool all over myself and didn't have the damn common courtesy to introduce themselves. I knew the doors were locked, and that this was a secure facility. The keypad on the door spoke to that idea. Sydney's 'take over the world' line was also a bit over the top. I've seen enough action movies to know that all of this stank of bad guys. Evil doers, enemies of good, whatever you'd like to call them. Bad guys is great in its simplicity though. Although a bit sexist. I had no doubt there were bad girls here too. Were they bad girls or bad bad girls. If you know what I mean. *Holy shit, wrong train again*, I thought as I shook my head to derail that one. The light seemed to turn off from the other side and my only guess was that whoever had been inside had left. This was my chance.

I jumped from the bed and headed for the door. It was, of course, locked. I knew it would be but hey, can you blame a guy for trying? I played with the keypad for a while, making no progress. I was by no means a double secret agent and had no idea what I was doing. Eventually, I headed back to bed. I lay in the bed, staring into the mirror as if it would somehow make me feel better. It didn't. Morning finally arrived, or whatever time was morning to these people anyway. Sydney entered, holding a plate of food. I smiled at her, and she smiled at me. As she placed the tray next to my bed, I grabbed her arm, probably too forcibly. The look on her very attractive face instantly changed from carefree to fearful. "Listen to me. I know what's going on." Her eyebrows furrowed in questioning. "This place. It's an observation room. People are watching me. Not good people either," I said, trying to get the point across. It worked. The dawning of realization crossed her face. "I need to get out of here and get back to my friends." She shook her head. "There is no getting out of here," she whispered back. "There is for me," I said. "No, I mean there is no way. There are guards in the hall, cameras, and we are underground. There is no way out," she said. "Help me," I whispered. She looked away. "We can help each other get out of here," I said, trying to get her on board. She looked back at me, her eyes glistening with what appeared to be tears. "I can't. They'll kill both of us if they catch us." "I can protect you. I'm a soldier," I told her. She thought for a long silent moment, neither of us moving. "Okay," she whispered. I let out the breath that I had apparently been holding in. "Thank you," I told her, letting go of her arm. She nodded. "I have to get back to work. I'll be back," she said, leaving the room in a flurry of motion, leaving the food tray behind. I ate hungrily, knowing that soon, I would hopefully need every ounce of energy available to make it out of here in one piece. The game was afoot apparently, and I just had to figure out when and how to strike. *Time for this action movie hero to breakout and kick some ass,* I thought to myself. Until then, it was time to rest up.

Several days had passed and Sydney had visited only one more time since our initial encounter that day. I was going stir crazy staying in this small stupid ass room. Even the toilet was in clear view of the mirror. I made sure to give them quite a show as I took several craps, making sure to assault their eyes and their ears to the best of my ability. When Sydney finally came back, she had somehow managed to get a hold of a loaded pistol. Entering quietly, she picked up the chart clipboard and read over it. She reached over me to check the IV bag to my left. The weapon was tucked into her waistband, and as she reached over me, with her breasts right up against my face, I felt it and pulled it out, handle first and slid it under my blanket. Granted, I almost missed the damn thing as my head was almost pressed air tight right against those magnificent boobies. Any man can attest that when boobies are in your face, the whole world seems to fade away. She blushed and quickly moved away, leaving the room without another word. A grin crept over her face as she left the room. I checked the pistol under the sheets of the bed, making sure prying eyes would not be able to see. If someone had been watching, they probably thought that I was jerking off or something after that whole event. Fine by me, no man would enter during private alone time. Ladies may not be so inclined, but it's man code to stay far far away until private time is concluded. I waited, and waited some more. Eventually, the door opened, just before lights out that day. She entered quietly, just as the light shut off. "The guards are having a shift change meeting, this is the best that I could do," she whispered. I had already been up, doing pushups in the corner of the room. Quite a feat with the stupid IV still in my arm. My robe was open and she took full advantage of that fact. I stood up as quickly as I could, covering what could now not be unseen. I dressed as quickly as I could, with her back turned to me as I did. In retrospect, even with her back to me, the mirror in the room made it easy to see everything that I was doing. "We should go," I told her, pulling the needle from my arm and covering it with a small bandage. She nodded. She placed her keycard against the reader and it clicked open. The hall was empty, with dimmed lights along the top and a clean hospital feel to it. It even had that weird sanitized smell. The ceramic tile was cold to the touch of my bare feet. I held the pistol in front of me and made my way out of the room, with her in tow. I looked to her questioningly. "Which way?" I asked. She pointed to the left. "This way." I again took the lead, and as we came to another intersection, a guard stood, obviously not paying any attention. "Is there any way around?" I asked her. "No, the other way is a dead end," she said. "Wonderful," I whispered. "Stay here," I said, holding the pistol behind me as I stumbled forward. The guard took notice and went rigid, his hand going to his own weapon. "Wuba luba dub dub!" I said out loud, almost at a shout. The look of confusion that crossed his face would have been absolutely hilarious, had I not been trying to save my own life. To be honest, I was scared shitless. I stumbled again, almost falling. The man ran forward, his hand pistol free. As he made it to me, I punched him square in the chin with my empty hand. I would love to say that he flew back from my almighty powerful hit. Instead, he took two steps back and looked at me with a mix of confusion and anger. I rushed forward and punched him a second and third time until finally, the shit went down. I pulled his pistol from his holster and handed it to my companion. "Let's go," I told her. We entered a stairwell and spotted two more guards making their way down to our level. "I guess the meeting is over," she whispered. "Do you think?" I whispered back, a bit perturbed. The look that she shot me would have melted me had I been paying any damn attention. I shot twice, and the two men hit the ground. The sound of the gunshots was loud in the stairs. "Time to run!" I told her as we took the stairs upwards. It was maybe a whole thirty seconds before I could hear what sounded like a hundred footsteps coming in from behind us. It was probably closer to a dozen men but sound is funny in confined spaces. You never really know what you're up against when sound is all that you have to go off of. We made it up two floors before another guard came across us. This one had apparently been waiting for us and he caught me a bit off guard. As we rounded a corner, he tackled me. It was a great tackle; I would give him that. We wrestled on the ground for a moment before I was able to get a good grip and I pushed him off of me, kicking him in the groin. *Poor guy*, I thought as I took in gasps of air. I had noticed two things while I tried to suck in oxygen. One was, there was no alarm. An escaped prisoner should have been an all hands-on deck event. Secondly, Sydney had not helped me at all, not even raising a finger, let alone her pistol. *What the hell?* I asked myself as I stood and dusted myself off. The guy on the ground had no weapon, and we left him behind, his cries of anguish receding behind us. We made it up two more flights until we came to a door marked 'exit'. *Yes! This was it!* I thought as I moved to the door. I could see a wide-open room with light at the end. It was definitely the way out. Footsteps could still be heard downstairs and the sounds of angry men was growing louder by the second. I pushed the door open and walked into the very spacious room. It felt and smelt like an aircraft hangar. There were crates and equipment piled up in different sections and a man standing directly in my path. I approached him, with my weapon at the ready. "Hello, Mr. Barnes," the man said. "Hi guy," I said, keeping my eyes trained on him. "How does it feel to have freedom almost in your grasp?" he asked. As I came closer, it was apparent that this was a military man. A General apparently. "It feels dandy, truth be told," I said. He smiled. "I just wanted you to get a taste of that before the real fun begins," he said. I stopped my advance. It took my mind just a moment longer to process what he had said than it should have. "Sorry, say what now?" His smile grew. "You are about to undergo a grueling set of tests and frankly, it's always better to remove the ideas of escaping early on so that you're more pliable during the process. "The hell I am," I said, standing up straighter. "Yes, the hell you are. In fact, you'll be helping us out greatly. You are subject #1 in an ongoing test to see the effects of continuous infection for an immune." My eyebrows shot up. "Immune?" I asked, the other questions and statements in my mind quickly vacating to make room for this new information. "Indeed. Apparently, you are one of the lucky few who have bonded with the infection in a way that defies our knowledge. You turned, but only for a very short time period. In fact, by the time that you arrived here for study, you were back to normal. It was fascinating," he said, his eyes lighting up with excitement at the possibilities. "Well, I really do appreciate the getting me back on my feet and all of that but I hate needles and I don't play well with others, so I think it's time I call it a day and head on out of here," I said, as I stepped forward again, hoping to get by the uniformed man.

A door to my right opened with a loud clang and eight men entered, holding batons. I grinned, and turned to train my pistol on them. Without a second's hesitation, I fired half a magazine into the group. A funny thing happened though. It didn't do anything at all. The men all stood there, smirking back at me as if I was on some kind of prank show. I looked down at the gun in my hands. Smoke was coming from the barrel and it had definitely fired. "You've been using blanks, I'm afraid," the man said. I pulled the pistol around for good measure and fired a round his way. The action did, in fact, catch him off guard, and he took a step back, recoiling slightly. I stood there, puzzled. The gun was given to me by Sydney. I turned to her. She stood, with both hands in her pockets, watching everything unfold like it was a damned dinner show. "Really?" I asked her. She shrugged. "You're not the first mildly attractive guy that has tried to get out of here. There's not much point to hurt my career for a nobody like you," she said. To be honest, I was a bit taken aback. "Mildly attractive? I think I'm drop dead gorgeous, thank you very much," I said, a bit appalled at her choice of words. "Besides, your hair looks stupid," I said, the feeling of betrayal growing inside of me. In retrospect, I could have gone with something more meaningful and less childish but at that point, my mind was drawing a blank. She punched me right in the stomach and I let out a weird, wheezing noise as I hit the ground. The men closed the distance and formed around me, and I began to receive one of the worst beatings that I ever had the pleasure of receiving. I think it was actually top two. The whole while, the General guy and Sydney stood, watching every hit with those hard, plastic batons. Finally, after a good long whopping, I passed out.

Chapter Nineteen

I woke up feeling like absolute shit. It was as if every inch of me had been spanked repeatedly with a metal paddle that was designed to tenderize meat. So much so that as I laid there with my eyes open. I felt that I was unable to move. This was not the first time that I've felt like this to be sure. The helicopter crash, then the Humvee crash. This was the first massive beating that I had ever had though. I decided while enjoying the pain and lying there, that this beating took first place after all. Poor Brenda and her friends in 3rd grade. They'd no doubt be saddened to hear someone out beat those playground thugs. I hated fights my entire life and I had always been one of those people that tried to avoid conflict whenever possible. Sure, sometimes, it made an argument much more difficult here and there, but I was always a lover and not a fighter if you know what I mean. While I laid there, I surveyed my surroundings. I was back in my observation room. *Interesting choice*, I thought. *I would have not put myself back into the same room.* One thing was plainly different though. I couldn't move. I thought it had just been from the shooting pain of probably a couple of dozen bruises and cuts, but as I looked at myself in the room's large mirror, I saw the straps along my chest, wrists and feet. *Kinky*, I thought, sighing to myself as I closed my eyes once again. The best thing for my injuries, I knew, was rest. I obliged, falling fast back into sleep. It was who knows how long before I was violently pulled from my dreams. I felt a throbbing in my arm as I woke up and looked down. There, to my consternation, was something that was not there previously. It was another I.V. The needle was protruding from my arm and it was connected to a tube that led to a machine to my left. It was drawing blood, not providing me with lifesaving liquids. Not a drop of blood, mind you, a lot of blood. The wave of nausea hit me hard as I watched it drain. I can cut through a dozen infected, watching their blood and guts spill all over the floor and I can handle that with no problem. This though, was something I had a hard time stomaching. I was bleeding my own blood, and it was gross. A memory sparked into my mind and try as I might, I could not stop the inevitable flashback.

Before the zombapoc, when my then wife and I had conceived our first and only child, I was not able to deal with that blood either. The first time we had seen a midwife and they had to draw blood, I almost passed out. "Are you alright?" the nurse had asked, glancing over my way. Apparently, I had turned two shades whiter than normal. "Yeah," I somewhat blurted out, trying to keep my eyes on anything except what was going on directly in front of me. "Honey?" my wife had asked, with a hint of concern in her voice. "You two just do you, I'm good. This picture is fascinating, that's all," I said, staring at a photo with instructions on good hygiene habits and what infections they help avoid. It really was not fascinating at all, but it seemed to work to get their prying eyes off of my face. It wasn't until the car ride home that the wife asked me about it again. "So what happened today?" she asked. "Whatever do you mean?" I asked back, already knowing where the conversation was heading. "You looked like you saw a ghost," she replied. "I'm just not good with blood," I said back. She looked at me. "I've literally seen you wrap someone's bloody hand after they cut themselves with a knife." She was referring to a family get together that had happened a year earlier. One of my uncles was attempting to show off his cutting skills when he ended up slicing his hand from wrist to finger. I put pressure on it, and wrapped it and proceeded to drive him to the ER. She was right though, that did not bother me at all. "I guess this is different," I told her. "Why?" "Well, because I love you and seeing someone I love's blood just made me sick," I said. "Aww you love me?" she said, mocking me a little. "Yes babe, so let's just move past this okay? I can build a house but not see your blood, so let's call it even." She laughed. "Alright honey, just remember that we have appointments all the way up until after the baby is born. You might have to get used to it." "Nah, I'll just bring a book next time." She again laughed, and so had I, looking into her beautiful eyes as we headed home that day. That had been one of the last times that we had had a decent conversation, before our marriage had burst into flames and I was left dealing with the ashes.

It was that thought that brought me back out of my flashback. The damn machine was still on, this time, Sydney was by my bed. “Look what the cat ate, threw up and then dragged in,” I said quietly, with my voice still suffering from what could have only been a punch to my throat. I sounded awful, like I had been gurgling glass. She ignored me, and went about checking the different instruments in the room around me. “I can’t believe I fell for it. You’re a class act,” I said again, trying to get a rise out of her. She removed part of the IV, creating a pick line to be used without having to reinsert a needle over and over again. My guess was, they had much more planned for me and this was just out of convenience, not out of any care towards me. After pulling the cartridge of blood from the machine, and sealing it, she finally looked into my eyes. “You are one of five people that I am observing and testing in this facility. All five of you have obvious signs of being bitten and infected, but do not show obvious outward symptoms. This could be attributed to slow turning, or it could be some kind of resistance. You could all also be carriers of the virus. Either way, it's invaluable data that will help elevate me to a level that would allow me to get out of this job and into a position where I never have to touch another patient ever again. I'd get to rub elbows with the elite here and never deal with bed pans ever again. I don't see much incentive to do away with all of that when all I have to do is play along," she said. I just stared at her. "Have a good night, Mr. Barnes." She closed the door and turned off the light, leaving me, once again, in pitch darkness.

Great, I thought. *Now I've got to pee.*

Chapter Twenty

Rachel had driven half way through Albuquerque, stopping at a now defunct mall. The Coronado mall had done a marvelous job before the fall of adapting to the changing retail atmosphere. Utilizing their insane amount of parking spaces, they leased out parts of the lot for new restaurants and small businesses. Inside, they had new and exciting service-based businesses to draw new customers in. It legit had a bowling alley and arcade, as well as a high-end Cheesecake Factory. In its day, it was a ton of fun to explore the place and see the sights. Now, the mall was an empty shell of its previous existence. The few random cars in the assorted parking lots stood as reminders of past Christmas rushes and summer hangouts. The small group pulled into a handicap stall, just outside of the entrance with a Barnes and Noble at the corner. Once the Humvee was parked, Rachel sat, staring out the windshield. Tears were falling from her face, and she began to shake. The grief of the events of the past hour beginning to weigh heavily on her. "Lady, you know you're in a handicap spot, right?" Cara said, poking Rachel's shoulder. Even in the midst of utter despair, a smile crept onto her face and as she cried, she laughed. "Yeah, you're right. I don't think anyone will mind. If anyone shows up, and wants this spot, we'll move. I promise," she said, which seemed to placate the young girl. Cara smiled contently and sat back into her seat. Rachel looked around at the other occupants of the vehicle. The kids were jovial, not worried in the slightest about what had just transpired. The adults though, were sullen and looking out their nearest window. "Are we going back?" Jaylin asked. "Bet your ass we are," Rachel replied, her grief slowly turning to determination. "Everyone, let's get out and stretch for a second," she said, in no time at all, every occupant filed out. They did as suggested, stretching and breathing in the fresh cold night air. The scent of the rain was still present with each inhale. "Can we do a group hug before we go?" Cara asked.

The little girl was definitely starting to grow on the group. "Yes honey, I think that's a great idea," Jaylin said, her voice changing to that motherly voice that all women seem to have innately built in. At the little girl's direction, they all came together and had a big hug fest. Even Cayden, who tried to avoid all things touchy feely joined in. After a minute or so, the moment ended and everyone piled back into the Humvee. "Ladies, are you ready for a rescue?" she asked, letting the glow plugs warm up and starting the vehicle. She looked in the rear-view mirror and saw each woman nod confidently one by one. "Alright then. Let's do this," she said as they pulled out of the lot and headed back the way they had come.

Thirty minutes later, they found the street that led to the target house. Something was different this time. Even in the rain, a haze was visible as they turned off of Tramway Boulevard and onto the residential street. As they neared, they saw the reason for it. The house that they had just defended and escaped from was burning. The entire house was engulfed in flames and burning zombies still surrounded the building. They were falling to the ground around the inferno, their skin literally melting off of them as they stood around it like some kind of perimeter fence. The group of survivors stayed back, away from the blaze and watched the house burn. They waited, hoping to see some sign of their friends. Minutes ticked by with no change. Nothing, except the flickering of flames through the house, and flailing zombies as they succumbed to the fire. They sat, with the engine idling as the supports for the home finally gave out and it crumpled to the ground, collapsing like a house of cards. The fire outside matched the fire in the women's eyes as they all watched the house take its last breath. They had lost three friends. Kenneth, a man whom they all had grown to love and admire. A soldier and protector. Atencio, the witty, sarcastic comedic relief. Ashmore, the only trained medic in their group, and an attitude to match. They were gone, just like everything else seemed to be in this world now. The ashes of the house seemed to resonate with the group. Their hope for rescuing their friends was diminished in every way. Rachel pulled the Humvee away, driving up and down every connecting street, hoping for some kind of sign. None came. Their friends were gone, and nothing that they could do would fix that. The Humvee signaled near empty for fuel. Dawn began to approach and the clouds began to clear. It was going to be a sunny day. That fact did not help in the survivor's deposition at all. The fuel gauge hit E and they made the decision to abandon the search. They had to refuel and head back home. If nothing else, they would deliver the children safe and sound. At a cost of four adults and two children, they would give these two kids a future. They terminated the search and headed back to the interstate. She knew there were several gas stations in the area that she hopefully could refill the fuel tank at. The zombapoc happened so fast that many gas stations had not been drained dry. Everyone had made a mad dash out of the city, dropping what they were doing and leaving with only what they had on them in most cases. As the smoke trail in her rear-view mirror slowly diminished, she once again began to cry. This time, she let it out. The rest of the occupants shortly followed suit. As they drove on, the sound of unbearable grief was the only sound that could be heard besides the near constant beating of the rain on the hood as they drove forward.

Chapter Twenty-One

Somewhere around 8-10 hours had passed while I was tied to the bed. It was not nearly as kinky as I had previously imagined. In fact, I pissed myself. I'm not too ashamed of that fact now. Honestly, who wouldn't just let go after hours of holding it in? These people holding me prisoner now had a mess to clean up and who would have the last laugh then? *Probably them*, I thought as I lay there with the cold wet sheets under me. For hours more, I lay there, contemplating the answers of life. Finally, the door opened, with Sydney and two guards entering and heading directly for me. I did have a small measure of satisfaction when she received a whiff of the now hours old pee. She crinkled up her nose and I could not help but smile. She saw my smile and jabbed me in the gut. I let out a small cry of pain, the smile effectively wiped off of my face. “I hope you're comfortable. We’re going to give something new a try,” she said. She signaled to the two men around her, who also received their fair dose of my smelly goodness. One of them, the taller of the two, set a small briefcase-type container on the table next to my bed. They then both proceeded to grab my arms and legs. “Is this really necessary guys?” I asked the two men. “If you want a hug, just get one. I won’t tell anyone and I am a gentle lover,” I whispered in a sensual voice. The corner of the shorter man's lip began to quirk upwards in the faintest hint of a smile. He was a black man with a tattoo visible on his right arm. As I glanced over it, I saw the same tattoo on the other man's arm as well. My guess was some kind of brand. “Hey man, nice tat,” I told him. He got serious really quick. “Shut up,” he responded. The taller man, a white fellow dug his elbows into my mid-section as he held me. “Wow, hey thanks for that. Did you two get those tattoos on a couple’s night out or something?” I told him. “Do you ever shut the fuck up?” Sydney said, apparently not entertained. “Why do you ask?” I said, looking at her quizzically. While I had conversed with my two associates in the room, she had retrieved a syringe. Besides being bigger than one, I imagine would be used for horses, its contents are a mystery to me. The black and green liquid inside completely out of my realm. It wasn't until I really thought about it that it came to me. I looked straight into her eyes. "Are you fucking serious?" I said, the fear beginning to truly well up in me. She grinned in response. "You're a smart man. We've tried to identify some kind of resistance but as of yet have come up empty. We're going to see if you are resistant to the infection, or truly immune. This here is a healthy dose of the virus, mixed with a cocktail of other drugs. You're going to go night night and while you're out, we're going to see what this does to you. Is there anything that you'd like to say in possibly your last few minutes of life?" she asked. I thought long and hard on that question. The world around me seemed to stop, or at least slow down. I looked back up and met her gaze. "When this is all over, I'm going to kill you." She smiled and plunged the syringe into my IV line. "That's what I thought you'd say," she said as I felt a mix of things all at the same time. I felt the warmth of what I can only assume was a pain killer.

That was surprising in itself, why the hell use a painkiller on a prisoner? Then I was hit with this immense pain that I could not describe, even at gunpoint. My back arched and I screamed. The two men holding me were almost flung off as I writhed in pain. I could feel the liquid flowing through my arm and into the center of my body. As I screamed in agony, my eyes roamed the room. In the doorway, watching attentively was the General that I had met just recently. He was watching with incredible interest. "I'm....going...to..kill...you...too," I told him, through clenched teeth as another wave of pain tore through me. Sweat was pouring off of me as my temperature spiked to past fever levels. I looked into the mirror as what must be the night night juice finally began to do its job. As I stared at the mirror, I saw my eyes slowly begin to turn a dark brown and then a black. *I was turning.* "No!" I screamed as my body finally collapsed and I faded into pain-filled darkness.

Chapter Twenty-Two

The small band of survivors fueled up at a nearly destroyed Smith's fuel station off of Central and Tramway. The site had previously been a large grocery store, with a strip mall opposite to it. The entire area was devoid of nearly anything useful. Even the diesel that they got had to be siphoned from other vehicles and not from the pumps as they too were surprisingly dry. It took hours to fill the tank that way, but the group did it diligently. It helped to temporarily distract them from their losses. Once the tank was full, they proceeded unceremoniously out of the city, heading back the direction that they had come. Hours of driving, hours of sitting in a pile of grief taller than any building they had ever laid eyes on. Eventually, they made it back to Cannon AFB with no real issues. In fact, the trip had been completely uneventful. *Go figure*, Rachel thought. *Only when we've lost half our team does something finally go right.* Even when they pulled through the previous gun battle zone from their first trip, there was neither a single hide nor hair of anyone in their way. They pulled up to the heavily fortified gate of the base. A small squad of four soldiers, in full combat gear surrounded the Humvee with their weapons trained on the occupants. One of the soldiers, a Sergeant Weed, stepped forward and peered into the rolled down window. He recognized Rachel almost immediately. His eyes glanced around to the other occupants of the vehicle. "Where is the rest of your team?" he said. Rachel put her hands down and began to cry. Sgt. Weed sighed aloud. He waved to the rest of the squad to stand down. He looked back in at Rachel. "All arrivals have to check in with medical. Get checked up and see Captain Dail. I'm sure he'd like a debriefing," he said as he moved out of the way. The gate opened, and the vehicle rolled through. A group of mechanics at the motor pool stared as the blood-encrusted, dented Humvee came to a stop. One of the headlights was out, and unimaginable parts of bodies still stuck to the grill. The mechanics watched as the occupants got out, grabbed their gear and headed to the medical wing. Once the passengers were out of sight, they did a quick 'not it' routine of touching their noses until the last man out had the unenviable task of washing the exterior of the vehicle. An older man, Johnny, didn't get the bit and ended up the man for the job. He spent the next six hours scrubbing the living hell out of that vehicle, muttering at what bullshit it was. *What did I do in a previous life to deserve this shit?* he thought as he pulled a middle finger from a gap in the front quarter panel. He looked at it, and laughed.

The proceedings at the medical wing progressed quickly. Each one of them were checked for bites, and other infections. The two children received their first hot shower in months. The rest of the crew took the time waiting for test results to catch up on sleep. Sleeping in a safe place was becoming more and more rare. It was an unfortunate side effect of the apocalypse, like so many other things that had previously been second nature. The good old days of cruising down Route 66 with the top down, the wind blowing in their hair, without any cares in the world were long gone. 12 hours later, the group was assembled and led into Capt. Dail's office one at a time to present a debriefing. By the time that was finished, they were once again exhausted. Reliving the events of the past few days and the trauma of losing their own weighed heavily on each of them, Rachel more than most. She sat through the whole affair, her tone of voice almost robotic as she added more and more information to the captain's file. When their meeting was over, he stood and embraced her. The scene was not by any means normal military protocol, but then, what was anymore? He held her and she cried, the pain washing over her once again. This man had been their mentor and knew just about everything about each of them. He knew their hopes, their dreams and their passions. She realized then though, that their loss was also his. He had lost members of his team, his children, if you will. She looked up to his face, the clean shaven, perfectly groomed face and saw tears of his own falling. This new world was exactly that, a new world. After several moments, they parted and she left the office, thanking him quietly. Slowly, she made her way through the complex and to the bunk rooms.

The majority of the survivors on base lived in makeshift housing built by the Air Guard Red Horse Unit. When the shit hit the fan, they were able to mobilize much quicker than most units and had the highest percent of survivors in the remaining US arsenal. Two of the soldiers, a Staff Sergeant Garduno and a Senior Airman Marin walked down the hall, heading for the briefing room. The two women were inseparable since basic training, and it showed. Rachel stared at the floor as she walked onwards and ran directly into the two women on their way to brief before guard duty. The three women ended up tangled on the ground in a mess of arms and legs. Countless apologies insured. The two women though, once up and looking at the woman before them knew instantly that something was wrong. Women have an uncanny ability to sense things like that. The two airmen embraced Rachel in another hug. The fact that she did not know them in the slightest did little to discourage the hug. Once they separated, they introduced themselves. "I'm Cassandra," said the shorter of the two women. Both were around 4'11 or so and could have been sisters. The just a half an inch taller of the two pointed to herself, "I'm Natalie," she said. Rachel shook their hands. "Rachel," she said. "We're off to guard duty, would you like to come?" Cassandra asked. "I think I'm just going to get some rest," Rachel replied. "Oh okay. Well then, come join us for breakfast at least," Natalie said. "I have so much stuff to do," Rachel trailed off. "Great, we'll see you at breakfast!" Cassandra said, cutting her off. "Yeah girl, see you then!" Natalie piped in, stopping Rachel from declining the request. She nodded in reluctant surrender. The last thing that she felt like doing was having some attempt at casual conversation, but she knew deep down that these two women would not let her say no. The two airmen said their goodbyes and Rachel found her bunk. The room felt empty, and so did her bed. She, of course, knew why. Her other half was gone. Not only that, but she had lost over half of the only people that she considered friends left in this world. *This destroyed, stupid world,* she thought. She removed her boots, and stripped down, slowly looking around the room as she did so. The tiny room, barely a bedroom by most people's standards was as empty as her heart, and just as cold. As she laid her head to rest once again, her mind wandered. The memories of the good times and the bad times, thoughts of hope and those of despair. After hours of restlessness, she finally fell into sleep.

Her alarm awoke her the next morning. It felt to her as if it had only been minutes since she had fallen asleep. The dreams had turned to nightmares and had taunted her through a vast majority of the night. She felt stiff; her muscles still tense with the adrenaline slowly receding through her veins. She stood and dressed in the same clothes that she had dropped on the floor the previous night. Two fucks were less than what she gave life at that point. She walked down the halls, the route all too familiar. After using the restroom, she made her way to the chow line. To her surprise, the two women were there, waiting for her. "Well, it's about damn time," Natalie said, pointing to Rachel. Cassandra turned in response and both airmen made their way over to her.

"We've been waiting for you. Let's get some grub," she said, taking Rachel by the arm. They led her over to the line and proceeded to fill her plate with the assorted food. Rachel was not hungry and felt like she never would be again, but that would not stop the two from piling it on. An open table was close by and the two women surrounded her. Each took turns asking her questions. Slowly, she began to come out of the horrible shell of misery that she had been encased in and told them her story. The ups and the downs, the love and the pain. The two women listened patiently, each fascinated and then devastated by the turn of events. After spilling what felt like her life story, and receiving another round of hugs, the two airmen told her their stories, and for just a little while, she was lost in something other than her own agony.

Chapter Twenty-Three

Natalie began first. "The two of us," she pointed to her and Cassandra, "We were freshly back from serving in Europe. No combat, mind you, but it was definitely educational. We didn't have much to do while we were there, so we spent most of the time visiting local hotspots. We visited Paris and had a crap ton of parties on our time off." "Good times," Cassandra threw in. Natalie nodded. "When the outbreak started to ravish the United States, most of the military was recalled from abroad. Our tour was cut short and our unit was thrown onto a couple of Globemasters." Rachel looked questioningly at the two women. "They're these massive planes that the Airforce used to transport troops and goods around the world," she clarified. Rachel nodded her understanding. "So anyway, we found ourselves recalled.

When we landed in the good US of A, shit was already going crazy. We landed, and immediately refueled. We weren't on the ground for very long before we began to have stragglers coming from a damaged portion of the fence line and heading for us. We had seen the news and we saw the writing on the wall. We took up tactical positions around the plane and fired on any of those things heading our way. Other planes around us were constantly landing or taking off." Cassandra nodded, "It was a damn madhouse," she said. Natalie continued, "We were one of the last flights that made it out of there. The base was overrun shortly after. We zigzagged across the US as one base granted us permission to land only to revoke it as they too came under attack. Our pilot and some of what was left of our brass made the decision to head for home. Cannon AFB was our destination and when we landed, it was actually quite peaceful. In fact, everything looked normal. We, of course, expected the worst. The base commander met us on the tarmac, and welcomed us with open arms. They had been fighting off small groups of infected and were low on staff, and so we filled in. Almost all of us were trained engineers and having the knowledge of how to build.." "Or blow up," Cassandra cut her off. "Yes, or blow up damn near anything," Natalie grinned as she continued on. "We came in handy. Now we are the brains behind all of the new buildings going on around the base," she said proudly. Rachel nodded, remembering just how many new buildings or contraptions had been built since their initial arrival. Cassandra spoke, "I miss the hell out of Netflix. It was the best lover that I ever had," she said, Rachel looked at her in puzzlement. "Guys are trash lovers and Netflix was always there for me," Cassandra said, a broad smile across her face. Rachel smiled, something that she had not done in days. "That took forever, girl," Cassandra said, commenting about her smile. Rachel shrugged, her smile fading. "We get it. You've had a rough go of it. So from now on, you'll be having breakfast with us and there is no way out of it so don't bother trying," Natalie said. Rachel simply shrugged again.

Eventually, breakfast was over. The two airmen went to bed and Rachel began her day. She reported to duty, but was told she would be off duty for several more days. She went to the bar, 'Ye olde Watering Hole' said the wooden sign mounted outside. The civilians had voted for that name apparently. When she entered, she was not surprised to see the place packed. Apparently, the end of the world was good for business. The base utilized a credit system for currency, where the engineers had figured out a way to produce cards with magnetic strips that would allow base personnel to add or subtract credits similar to a debit or credit card. That system enabled people to earn a living so to speak, while allowing the stability that currency afforded. If you didn't do the work, you didn't receive credits and you didn't eat. In the zombapoc though, everyone worked or they died. The drinks were cheap, as their raids to local stores had produced hundreds of cases of beer. No one wanted a belligerent, wasteful drunk walking around causing trouble, and so the alcohol was only allowed at the bar and the bartenders knew when to cut off the flow. If the scavengers found and brought alcohol back with them, they could sell it for credits to the bar, or drink it within the walls, and prices for the goods were based on availability and risk.

The harder it was to get something, the more it's worth. She found an empty seat, one of only two in the entire place and sat down heavily. A waitress asked for her order and placed it, and Rachel sat, looking around at the assorted tables. At most, jokes and stories were being told, creating a warm atmosphere at a majority of the bar. Mixed in though, she could see people like her, trying to drink away their nightmares or their memories. She received her beer, a tall cider. For those of you who don't believe that cider is 'real' beer, she would happily inform you that it generally has a higher alcohol content than most beers, and that by default, makes her beer manlier than any other. "Officer on deck!" someone in the crowd shouted, and every single soldier, sailor, airmen, and marine immediately stood at attention. That was mighty impressive, considering some were almost to the point of being drunk. Wobbling or not, they were standing as straight up as possible. "As you were," the figure said as he made it past the entrance and into the bar. Rachel had been one of those at attention and she slowly lowered herself back into her seat. The cider was on her table and as she took her first sip, she realized that the figure had stopped to her right. She glanced up and saw that it was the base commander, Johnson. She had only met him twice, once on their arrival to base and next when she was sworn in to serve. "Sir?" she made a move to stand back up, believing possibly that he wanted her seat. He waived his hand in a dismissive gesture. "I'm here for you," he said, coming to stand opposite of her. "For me, sir?" she asked, completely perturbed. "I was debriefed regarding your unsanctioned mission to Albuquerque for those children," he said, causing Rachel to move uncomfortably in her seat. Her eyes looked down at her glass as she took another swig. After a moment of awkward silence, she responded. "I'm sorry sir. We felt it was the right thing to do." His hard eyes softened ever so slightly. "I'm not here to chew you out. I'm here because I agree with your assessment." She looked into his eyes, completely shocked. "Thank you, sir," she said, almost stuttering it out. He smiled, it was the first time she had ever seen the man smile, even in passing or on events when he was off duty. "You did the right thing. Those kids needed help, and those kids are our future. If we have any hope of continuing the human race, we need to save and raise as many children as possible." Rachel nodded. "That is why I am here now. Every single member of your group attested to your level headedness, your ability to think on your feet, and putting the children's safety above yours and that of your team," he said. Rachel took a long pull from her beer. "Thank you sir, but I lost people." "That happens," he replied. "Any military leader worth their weight has lost troops. It's that first loss that provides wisdom to every decision after that. It makes us more careful, more involved. I have no doubt that's what it will do for you," he said. The crowd around them had quieted down as several tables of patrons had left. The time hit 8pm and lights out was at 9pm. There was a curfew between 10pm and 5am for anyone other than active guards as a safety precaution so most on base took the 9-5 hours to get their sleep in. "So if you don't mind my being blunt sir, you didn't come here just to compliment me, did you?" she asked. He smiled again. "Right on the nose. I am putting together a mission and I want you and your team involved." Her eyebrow raised in surprise. "I'm sorry sir, I don't think I'd do anyone any good right now." "I'm reassigning you so there is really no point in saying no, although obviously, I'd prefer if you were doing it because you want to." She sighed, finishing her beer. "Yes sir, I'm in." "Great. I thought you'd say that. Be at my office at 0915 for a read in," he said, paying for her drink and leaving the bar. She sat, and watched him leave. *What in the hell?* she asked herself as she looked at her watch and decided to call it a night, not having any clue in the slightest what the next day would hold.

The meeting started promptly at 0914 with Rachel, Jaylin, and Isabel standing on the opposite side of a large wooden desk. On the other side was the base commander and two other men Rachel had never seen. One was a very thin and tall man wearing a navy uniform and the other was an air force. "I'll start by thanking you all for being here. These two men have read through all of your files several times over, so I will cut to the chase and introduce who they are. This is Captain Ryan O'Guinn of the USS Mobile Bay," The man nodded slightly, "and this is Major Stephen Pendley of the Air Force's 6th Reconnaissance Squadron based out of Holloman AFB." He nodded as well. "Now that we are all acquainted, let's get started." He motioned for everyone to take chairs assembled around the room. The seats were by no means the plastic and metal ones littered around the base. These were the kinds that only the top dogs got to sit in; politicians and military officers. The leather chairs felt awkward to the group of women now sitting in them. Colonel Johnson opened a manila envelope and pulled out several photographs. He stood and hung each of them up on a bulletin board that was previously cleared of any information. It seemed rather out of place in his office. He tacked each one up, one at a time, before he sat back down. "The photograph on the right was taken by a surveillance aircraft operating in the New Mexico desert, several days ago." As the women studied the photograph, it was evident that it was a photograph of a black hawk helicopter completely painted in black camouflage. When he figured enough time passed, he moved to the next one. "The next photo is of the same helicopter just two miles south of this base." Sure enough, the black hawk had landed with what looked like several men in various states of entry into the aircraft as it sat on the sand. "The third photograph is of the helicopter landing at a previously unknown facility," he said. Rachel took all three pictures in, and then looked at the Colonel. He was staring right back at her. "Do you have a question?" he asked. "Yes sir." She took a deep breath, "Are these the ones responsible for our base sabotage over the past few weeks?" she asked. Major Pendley spoke up. "We've been able to identify signals coming from the facility that match those used by our aircraft software. It can be assumed that they have the ability to hack into some of our systems." "He means yes," Johnson said. "We also believe that there are a small handful of saboteurs within the base itself. Based on the amount of issues that our aircraft here have run into, both while operating and those still on the ground." "So what are we here for, sir?" Rachel spoke up again. "You are here because we are planning a joint operation to find out who is causing harm to my beloved base, our troops and why. We will find a way into the facility, and we will have a chat with whoever is responsible." He looked each of the women in the eye before proceeding. "We will have the support of the USS Mobile

Bay. The Captain here will have his ship parked along the Gulf of Mexico, just off of the coast of Texas. They are the only available naval support in the area, as the rest of the surviving fleet is still reorganizing itself. Inundated with refugees and low on supplies, their operational capabilities are severely limited. However, with the help of Captain O'Guinn, we will be able to rain down hell on the facility if for any reason we deem it necessary to do so." Major Pendley leaned forward. "Unfortunately, Holloman AFB was between training cycles and we did not have nearly the success as far as recalling personnel as the Colonel did here. We only have a half dozen pilots and four of our unmanned pilots remaining. We will be pooling our resources to transport a strike team to the facility. This will include two dozen hand selected personnel, of all branches. You three will be responsible for helping to select the rest of the ground teams and for assisting in the planning department, then entering the facility. You'll be working with a small group of other base members who each bring a different perspective. From medical, to our tech guys to our engineers, you all will have a say in how this goes down." Rachel looked at the other two women in the room. It was, of course, a huge task, and one not to be taken lightly. Looking into their eyes though, she could see the same level of determination as was in herself. "We're in, sir," she said, and the two women nodded behind her. "Great," Johnson said as he stood up, "Head to the briefing room to meet the other members of your team." The other two officers both nodded to the group as they left the room. Once the door was closed behind them, all three men sat. Johnson let out a breath and pulled out a bottle of Glenlivet Scotch, and three glasses. Placing them on the table and filling each one three fingers. "Are you going to tell them?" the Major asked. Johnson pulled out the last photo in the envelope and stared at it long and hard. "Not yet. They've got a job to do." The photo being placed back into the envelope was a zoomed in shot of Shepherd being loaded into the same black hawk as the squad in all black before it arrived at the facility in the New Mexico desert.

Chapter Twenty-Four

Ken watched the small group drive away and a majority of the horde of infected give chase. They would never catch up, he knew and as the tail lights pulled away, he sighed deeply, knowing that his friends and the children were now safe. He turned back from the window and looked into the eyes of the others in the room. Atencio and Ashmore were the only ones left with him. They too had watched the Humvee drive off. The infected playing around at the door had tapered off with the vehicle leaving. He peered back down at the driveway below and saw two dozen or so still standing around below them, between them and the way they had come. Jumping from the window now was out of the question. If any of them suffered any type of injuries, they would be quickly overtaken, and it would be tough to outrun any of the fast infected in the middle of the night. After a fair bit of discussion, they sat on the carpeted floor of the bedroom, resting while they could. As if somehow the undead below knew that that was exactly what the survivors were doing, they, once again, began their assault on the door. From a light tap tap tap on the wood to an all-out beating with many fists. It once again began to shake, and cracks were widening. "So, what's the plan?" Ashmore said quietly. "We can try to find a way out of this mess or go down with the ship in a blaze of glory." "The second one doesn't sound like very much fun," Atencio muttered. "You really only like to do fun things, don't you?" Ken asked her. "Well yeah, who doesn't?" He shrugged. "I'm glad that everyone else got away at least," he said. "Yeah, but it doesn't do us much good right now, does it?" Atencio responded. Ken looked at her, "No, it doesn't, but isn't that worth something to you?" he asked, anger flaring up within him. She met his gaze, "Of course, it is. I'm glad they made it too, but I don't know about you, I would have much rather made it out with them than sitting in this cold ass room, surrounded by zombies that want to eat me, in what could quite possibly be my last few minutes alive," she raised her voice as she finished the last sentence. Another loud crack from the door was the only response. "So, what's the plan?" Ashmore asked once again. Kenneth stood and stretched, taking stock of what was in the room. Several candles were arranged on a night stand, the bed having been pushed aside in the rush to get to the window. A small closet that would barely fit one of them was off to the left side. Standing and walking to it, he opened it, finding 18 pairs of women's shoes and one pair of men's. That caused a smile to form on his worn face. A bottle of liquor was stashed under a pile of clothes in the very corner of the closet, as if one of the two former roommates were hiding it from the other. He grabbed it and looked it over. It was a bottle of cheap vodka. *Maybe we can just get wasted before we die*, he thought, but pushed it to the back of his mind. He placed the bottle on the bed, closed the closet and then went to the dresser. Inside, he found a wide assortment of clothing, and the ever-present parental toy drawer. If you're not sure what a toy drawer is in an adult's bedroom, you will someday. Nothing is more exciting to a married adult than play time. There was nothing of real value, other than a box of caramel cake mix and its partner, a tub of frosting stashed under several well used t-shirts. What the hell was cake mix doing in the drawer? Try as he might, he could not comprehend it, but he still tried, standing stock-still staring at the drawer for several minutes before finally shaking his head and closing the drawers. *People are so weird,* he thought. Walking back to the two women who were also now standing up, checking their weapons and slowly reloading magazines. "We need to get through the mass of zombies if we want to get out of here," Ken said. "Any ideas?" he asked the duo. They both shook their heads. Ashmore then stopped and looked at the bed and the bottle now laying on it. "Why don't we burn them out?" she asked. "Huh?" Atencio asked, completely confused. "Burn the fuckers out. Use fire to clear us a path?" "Where do you see any fire here?" Atencio asked her, still in confusion. Ashmore walked to the bed and held up the nearly full fifth of liquor. "Molotov anyone?" she said with a grin.

With a loud whoosh, they dropped the Molotov onto the grass just to the side of the driveway. The unwatered dead shrubbery quickly caught and spread the fire like a true forest fire would be proud of. The infected slowly began to migrate over to the flames, as if they were entranced by it. They didn't seem to mind as their skin began to smoke and literally melt off of their bodies. The skin began to drip off of those closest to the fire, with muscle becoming visible. The white tendons followed shortly thereafter. The fire moved up one wall of the house, following the long dead vines that had once been absolutely beautiful to the former homeowner. Infected from all around the house converged and stood, watching the flames dance as they burned alive. *Wait, is that even accurate? If they're dead, can they burn alive?* Ken asked himself as he watched. A breeze swept into the open window and the smell of burning flesh washed over them. There was definitely a hint of that bacon smell, but it was followed by the smell of burning clothing and burning shit. Literally, burning shit. Then the crackling of burning wood quickly assailed their ears. "That worked well," Ken said, high-fiving Ashmore. "Now what?" Atencio asked. "We wait. Does anyone have any cards?" he asked, sitting back down.

The fire quickly spread to the rest of the house, the heat and smoke beginning to rise into the bedroom. The pounding on the door had once again ceased. That was their cue. They, once again, stood and began walking to the door, moving what little leftover furniture that they had piled against it. Ken put his right eye to one of the bullet holes made by their previous attempts to keep the undead out. All of the remaining infected in the hallway were slowly moving across the hall and down the stairs to the first floor. "The fire is drawing them away," he informed the others as he watched. The trio began to sweat heavily as the floor under their feet began to heat up with the flames below. The smoke was beginning to become a physical presence, the dark cloud filtering through every crack in the wall and flooring around them. To avoid the obvious issues, they lowered themselves onto their knees to avoid the majority of the deadly air. "We're clear, let's go while the getting's good," Ken said as he opened the door.

Another dense blast of smoke and hair blew into the room. The hallway was littered with dead zombies, their heads and bodies destroyed in one way or another. Some had holes blown out of the back of their skulls, some with heads almost completely intact with the exception of an entry wound. Occasionally, bullets will be slowed enough to enter the skull but not exit, ricocheting around like the inside of a pinball machine. Not wanting to risk an accidental bite, the group placed their knees and feet carefully, staying as low to the ground as possible. As they neared the stairs, the heat from the fire hit them full force, causing a fresh intense sweat to begin to trickle down their foreheads and necks. At the bottom of the steps was the remaining infected that had been in the hall. Ken could tell this by the sheer amount of wood shards that were all over the clothing of the few infected in the rear. "We need to get through these guys and head for the back," he whispered to the others. They nodded in mutual agreement. He raised his rifle and fired. The zombie in the rear took the first round, the shot missing its mark but hitting it dead center in the spine, pun intended. It fell forward, paralyzed but twitching. The trio unleashed a wave of bullets into the zombies and assorted infected, pushing those in the front that had originally been staring into the gorgeous flames into said fire, creating more toasted and roasted Z's that were walking around like creepers at sunrise. For those of you gamers like Ken, that makes perfect sense.

When the path to the back door was finally clear, the small group made their escape, the glass door having previously been shattered during the initial zombie attack. Bloody broken shards littered the ground, adding a crunching sound to their foot falls as they erupted out of the burning home. Once outside in the chilled moisture filled air, they all gulped in large gasps of fresh air, coughing repeatedly as they did so. A half dozen infected were still heading their way from inside the house and in less than a minute, they were dispatched. Inside the home, a wall collapsed, causing the entire structure to lean to the right, and slowly, the once picture-perfect Albuquerque home fell in on itself, burying the remaining attackers inside of it. The place would be a tomb for an assload of undead, and unfortunately, of one child. The fire continued to burn, a spire forming as it licked over the previously pristine rooftop. They watched the house burn and saw the zombies and infected on the other side of the flames staring back at them. They didn't make any moves to cross the fire to attack. Instead, they stood in a Mexican standoff, the light around them dancing with each flame. Atencio and Ashmore were breathing deeply, laughing amongst themselves, thankful to be alive. Ken though, was perturbed. The special infected, the one that had dodged his shot was nowhere to be found. That fact bothered him to no end. He tried to spot the smelly bastard in the crowd beyond, to no avail. The rain that had taken a smoke break resumed its downpour, causing the fire before them to sizzle. It was time to go. The house was in the foothills of the Sandia Mountains, where the dozen trail heads were only as far as the backyards of most of the homes. "I think up is our best bet," he said, looking up at the looming mountain. "You want to hike all of the way up there?" Atencio asked. "When was the last time that we went for a nice nature walk?" Ashmore threw in, looking at Atencio. "I don't think that's a good idea," she said, trying to stomp out the plan. "I disagree. If we can reach the peak, there are a crap ton of antennas and we can probably use one of them to contact the base. If not, there are probably cars that we can use," he said, pointing upwards. It was, of course, too dark to see anything at all, so he slowly put his finger back down. "So we're going to climb however many miles to the top, use the towers to call for help and then sit tight?" Atencio asked, as she stood directly in Ken's face, meeting his eyes. At 4'9, she was feisty as ever, and he had to look down at her to meet her gaze. "Yep, that sounds about right. Or find a car," he said in response. "What about the fuel being bad? Or the battery?" she asked. He shrugged. "If we could get a car into neutral, we could roll it down the other side of the mountain far faster than we could walk." She stared at him, and he stared at her. "Okay, fine," she said, turning her gaze from his and beginning to walk to the gate in the yard. Beyond lay a pitch-dark mountain, with their only destination being the top of the behemoth in front of them. "Let's get this done," Atencio said as she took the lead, and up they went, the previously raging fire behind them beginning to slow its rage and calm as ash and embers formed at the feet of the zombies

watching their prey walk away.

Chapter Twenty-Five

"Good morning General, members of the board, and Praetor," Sydney said as she stood in front of a dozen men and women in a luxurious conference room. The marbled table, leather chairs and spacious interior added to the feeling of poshness. Even the lighting in the room had been meticulously chosen to show each seat in only the most flattering light possible. She was standing at the farthest side from the Praetor, with everyone else filling in seats on other sides between them. She was forced to stand, as she was not recognized as being a member of the council and not deserving of a chair at the head of power. Yet. "Good morning," many of the group relayed back, either with muttered responses or simple nods. The Praetor, of course, did not make a move nor acknowledge her with anything other than with his eyes. *He's such a dick*, she thought as she continued. "We initiated phase 2 of our testing using one of our subjects; a man recovered from a bite just outside of Albuquerque not long ago. As with the others, he appeared to be immune to the infection." She held out a small remote that lowered a projector from the ceiling above, to which everyone in the room turned to look at the display. "Subject 5 was physically fit, had no allergies or other medical issues, and was completely healthy. Other than the bite he had received, of course." Several slides showed him standing or sitting on the hospital bed, even one slide was taken in the hall during his perceived getaway. "You can see here," she paused, clicking to the next slide, "He was strong enough to take down several guards. This made him our prime candidate for expedited testing." The next photo was of the stairwell incident. "Once he was taken back to his room and restrained, we began testing in earnest," she said, clicking it again. On the screen was an assortment of charts and diagrams with medical information that a large majority of those in the room did not understand. She quickly dove into the data, showing everything from his weight and height to his blood sugar and heart rate. "As you all know from our previous briefings, I have been working on a concentrated dose of Serum 128…"

"Excuse me dear," an older woman spoke up, interrupting her mid-sentence. "We already know the serum works. The whole world is infected. Why are you still bothering with making it more concentrated?" she asked. "Yes Senator, the original virus worked like anticipated," Sydney said, taking a quick breath. "However, for the sake of our medical plans, we wanted to concentrate it to see if the patient is actually completely immune, or just simply resistant." The Senator nodded for her to continue. "What we found was something very interesting," she said as she clicked the remote again. On the screen, subject 5 was hooked up to a machine with a large batch of the black liquid feeding into his arm intravenously. His eyes were cloudy, his expression lifeless. "When we injected the subject with the original syringe, the effects wore off." The Praetor grunted. "Do you mean to tell me that he became uninfected?" he asked. "Yes sir. The infection spread through his body, and it changed everything from his eye color to his metabolism and his blood. After about 6 hours, the infection receded to the point where medically, he was fine." Gasps from around the table, and even a 'oh my god' came to Sydney's ears. Inwardly, she smiled. This is it, her time to shine. The General spoke up. "Are you saying his body is not only immune but he can cure the infection itself?" "Yes sir. I'm saying that if we keep him going, we could even have the basis for a cure. We would be able to produce it and control distribution of it." She smiled, and on the other side of the table, the Praetor smiled back. "This is just the beginning."

Deeper inside the facility, Shepard lay, heavily restrained. The near constant pumping of serum into his veins kept his body in an unknown state. It sat somewhere between life and death. His mind though heavily drugged was constantly battling the infection raging on. A battle of wills of the zombie virus against his human spirit. The question was, could he conquer the foe invading his body or would it overpower him for full control? Only time would tell.

Chapter Twenty-Six

Rachel, Isabel and Jaylin had spent the previous twelve hours delving into personnel manifests, files and other reports in their plans for the raid. Included in their group were several battle-hardened soldiers, a pilot, an engineer, a medic and a sailor for a total of ten. Overseeing the group was a Sergeant Elmsley. Elmsley was one of those that made it up the ranks by sheer tenacity. She didn't take any shit and always spoke bluntly, much to the consternation of some of her previous superiors. The group had made several lists and had come to conclusions on the entire mission personnel list, with her being the judge and jury for a majority of the choices. With a raiding party of two dozen, they would be split into small squads once the assault began, with the goal of infiltrating and capturing or destroying the rogue group in the desert. Rachel would be placed in the group on point, along with the two air guard members that she had met earlier, Cassandra and Natalie, Elmsley and the sailor Jewel. The sailor's job was to observe the raid and act as a radioman for the group. If they could not gain entry or things got too hairy, his radio calls to the USS Mobile Bay would result in the complete destruction of the facility from an assortment of cruise missiles. That, however, would not be preferable due to the amount of supplies, personnel and Intel that they could gain from a total takeover. Cassandra and Natalie's expertise from their time in Red Horse (Rapid Engineer Deployable Heavy Operational Repair Squadron Engineers were invaluable. The military loves their acronyms), gave them the special knowledge of demolition required from breaking through any doors that they could not bypass otherwise. Behind them would be the rest of the team, who would then spread out to take any other objectives as they arose. The best guess of the brass was that the facility was formerly a missile silo that was closed down and purchased privately. Thought to be abandoned after the sale, the basic layout of the silo system was fairly well known, however, the exact setup of the interior was up for debate. Much to the chagrin of the group, once inside, they would have to decide their next steps as they went. The military brass absolutely hated that idea but there were no alternatives. It was a vital objective and the assorted team members were going to take it, one way or another. The mission would commence two days later, and the raiding crew would be more than ready, or so they hoped.

Chapter Twenty-Seven

An hour after their initial start of their nature hike, Kenneth, Ashmore and Atencio made it up the well-used trail with the hope of making it to the top in three pieces. After their vacating the burning house of horrors, they had kept up their guard, with one of the group constantly looking behind them to see if any of the infected were following. None ever showed. As the hours of walking up hill took its toll, there was need to stop more and more often. "Can we stop?" Atencio said, frustrated. "Again?" Ashmore asked, nearly throwing her hands up in the signature 'I give up' way. "Yes, my feet hurt," she said, finding a rock nearly as tall as she was, and clambering up to the top. The petite woman proceeded to take off both of her boots and rub her feet. At her size, she looked like a child on a hike that her parents just had to take her with them. If it weren't for the camouflage pants and top, it would almost be a complete picture. “Fine, move over,” Ashmore said with a sigh. She too climbed the boulder and sat beside her friend. Or more than friend, or whatever. Kenneth, grumbling to himself, sat on the ground at the base of the large rock. “Damned women taking the good spots,” he whispered to himself as his ass hit the dirt. “What the hell did you just say?” Atencio nearly yelled. “Nothing shush!” he yelled back. Her evil eye finally left him as Ashmore caught her attention once again and they began to talk amongst themselves. Ken, with nothing to stimulate him, nodded off with his head resting against the rough rock. It was not the most comfortable pillow that he had ever had, of that there was no doubt, but in a pinch, it worked. His heavy eyelids closed and opened wide a half of a dozen times before they finally rested in the closed position.

It could have been only moments or even hours later that he was startled awake. His eyes opened wide and he dared not move a muscle. The two women were still talking above him, whispering and probably telling some crazy ass secrets about someone they hated or something. The hair on his neck began to stand straight up, and he felt that something just wasn't right. In the military, they describe the feeling of someone directly looking at you. They say that there is energy in it and when someone is looking right at you, your body, mind or soul somehow can feel that energy and it causes you to look at the person looking at you. Have you ever been at a restaurant, and seen someone that you think you recognize, so you stare at them, trying to confirm it? Then all of a sudden, they stop talking and look right back at you as if they somehow knew you were staring at them? That's what Kenneth was feeling right then, as if someone was staring intently at him, and as his eyes slowly scanned the area, they came to a rest on a patch of bushes up the trail and to their right. The sensation that he was feeling seemed to be coming from that direction. Slowly, his hand moved to his rifle that was laying by his right side. He kept his movements as slow as possible, with his eyes no longer looking at the bushes, to avoid putting energy back to the watcher. They teach that the best way to get around guards, and to sneak through parameters is to avoid looking directly at the guard, and using your peripheral vision instead. Many good soldiers died by not following the rule of thumb while trying to infiltrate an enemy encampment. As soon as his hand grasped the rifle, he lifted it and fired into the bushes, sending a three-round burst into it. The noise startled the women above him, causing Atencio to drop the shoe that she was still holding straight onto Ken's head, the steel toe boot causing him to wince with pain. He stood up, holding his rifle against his shoulder and keeping it trained on the now shredded plant life. A moment crept by, possibly two before a corpse fell to the ground from inside of the bush. Even from that distance, they could tell that something was strange. The corpse was pale, with unusually long nails on its outstretched hands. The ears too were larger than normal, with scratches all over its body, possibly from contact with the trees and cactus in the area. Atencio put her boot back on as quickly as she could. As she finished the last lace, the trees all around them came alive.

"Incoming!" Ashmore yelled as she fired into the trees to her right, Ken shooting directly ahead. Atencio pivoted, bringing her rifle up as two pale people came around the boulder, heading straight for the group. She fired on semi-auto, nailing the first one in the head, and the second in the chest. It fell away, clutching its chest as it did so. The group quickly huddled up and were soon back to back, taking shots as heads or figures popped out of the surrounding area. "Red!" Atencio shouted, Ashmore turning slightly for a wider angle of fire. The term 'Red' was in regards to her being out of ammo and needing to reload. Her fingers fumbled as she found the magazine release, placing the empty mag in her left pocket and pulling a full one out of her right breast pocket, feeling it slide into place in her rifle. Pulling the charging handle, she shouted "Green!" taking up her position once again in the firing line. Like a well-oiled machine, two dozen or so of the things were put down before the last round was fired just a minute or so later. The complete quiet in the night was deafening. With the smoking barrels of their weapons still hot to the touch, they moved forward as one, with Ken leading the pack. He came to one of the dead things on the trail and put his foot to it, confirming that it was, in fact, dead. "What the actual fuck?" he asked out loud as he bent down. The eyes of the man, for lack of a better word were weird. Weird, you ask? The eyes did not have the round pupil of a person, or the dead grey appearance of a zombie, but the eyes that you'd expect to see from a feline. It was something of the animal kingdom, not normal at all for humans. Ashmore pushed past, looking into the eyes with her pen light, and slowly tracing over the features of the thing. "Fascinating," she whispered. "It tried to kill us and you say it's fascinating?" Atencio asked her peevishly. Ashmore stood back up and looked her dead in her eyes. "Yes. I think this is a mutation," she said, staring at her whatever she was. Saying girlfriend would, while accurate, be weird without official confirmation, and Kenneth knew that men do not willingly step into a midfield like that without taking some serious damage. "So what are you saying?" Atencio spat back. "I'm saying that these things are obviously faster and stealthier than what we're used to, and they're seeing physical changes that would normally take thousands of years. The pale skin leads me to believe that they aren't usually in the sunlight, and may be nocturnal hunters. Their long nails point to that as well, no pun intended," she said. "The eyes also lead me to believe that they either have night vision or close to it," she concluded. Atencio audibly gulped. Ken signed. "Well, grab my ears," he said quietly. "Hunters," Ashmore said. "What did you say?" Ken asked, turning to look at her. "They're hunters. Infected with special abilities like these aren't something we should ignore," she said. "I think the name hunters fits just fine." A howl from what sounded like a dog or coyote in the distance behind them was cut off with a whimper. "I think it's time to go," Atencio said, pushing past the other two and speed-walking along the path up to the mountain's peak. "I second that," Ashmore said, following right on her heels. "I've got the rear, I guess," Kenneth said, following just two heartbeats after the duo.

Chapter Twenty-Eight

Five hours later, the trio made it to the end of the trail leading to the crest. Eight times over the course of the remainder of their hike, they had to fight off attacks from groups of hunters hell bent on having them for dinner, or a late-night snack depending on which one of them they got their long ass nailed claws into. The groups had been much smaller than the original bunch but that had not lessened the fear and terror of each encounter. Fast and silent infected jumping out at you in the middle of the night with no warning is enough to make anyone tinkle. Running horribly low on ammunition, and with all three of the survivors exhausted, they came across a visitor center/gift shop at the peak. The area had been closed off with only one or two cars in the entire parking lot. They walked through the barricades and after giving the front door some tender loving care with the butt of Ken's rifle, they entered. They began their sweep of the area. Inside was a beautiful array of artwork and nick nacks that you'd expect from a tourist spot, including rocks that you could buy by the bag. Ken wasn't sure at all who would buy a bag of rocks but hey, who was he to judge. One thing they had all caught upon entering was a smell. It was a smell almost any high school or college or whatever was above that athletes would recognize in a heartbeat. If you've ever been in a locker room with a bunch of sweaty people, you'd know the smell. It was the smell of dirty, unwashed bodies. It was definitely not the smell of decay like entering a home with several corpses piled up in the corner. They walked through the gift shop area, scanning for targets. Displays with an assortment of sweaters, t-shirts and jackets advertising the spot littered the room, with display cases around the perimeter. Off to one side was a door leading to an eating area, and a kitchen beyond that. Ken took the lead and went for the door. Opening it as quietly and slowly as was possible, he peeked inside. The smell of stinky people wafted up in force and he nearly let the door slam closed. Taking several deep breaths of clean (or cleaner rather) air, he moved into the room. The eating area was in disarray. Broken cans and jars were everywhere, with boxes smashed into small pieces mixed in. Visible footprints in the dust-covered floor instantly gave Ken the impression that someone had been here, and recently. He moved on, carefully monitoring where each step came down. The swinging door of the kitchen was next up and he opened the door just as slowly. Just as he was able to see inside, the barrel of his rifle was swept to the side as the swinging door burst open. He fell backwards, his finger pulling the trigger out of habit, sending two rounds into the ceiling and deafening all of them. The women had been right behind and raised their rifles to meet the new threat. Three hunters pushed and shoved each other through the doorway and towards the trio. One of them grabbed at Ken's shoe, attempting to pull him back inside of the room. "Hey!" Ashmore yelled out as the creature with the foot fetish looked up at her in response. "Eat this," she said calmly, putting a round through its nose. The other two had immediately leapt towards the killer of their friend, assuming that was the case and both landed within mere inches of Ashmore. Atencio was fast on the trigger, a three round burst peppering the side of the closest infected. The second one though, grasped at Ashmore's vest, sending both of them to the ground as it wrestled for warm food. Atencio could not take a shot safely without hitting her partner. She aimed, trying to find a spot to fire, with no success. Ashmore was trying to scramble backwards, putting as much distance between her attacker as possible. The hunter gained the upper hand, and was millimeters from taking a bite out of her neck, when its head was pulled back, and a loud crack was heard as Kenneth pulled its head to a horrible angle, breaking its neck. It fell, lifeless to the floor, its head landing on Ashmore's leg. She immediately recoiled and pulled away, standing up. "Jesus, that was close," she said, checking herself, wiping away a long trail of saliva from her neck, gagging in disgust. Atencio gave her an epic hug, and then checked her for bites as well. When they were clear, they reset, and took up positions around the room. Ken also reset from the near-death encounter and walked into the room that he was previously denied entry from. Inside was an absolute mess. The creatures had been staying here, of that he had no doubt.

Besides the stink, more cans and boxes were piled up in the right corner, completely empty. The pantry was completely cleaned out of anything edible. It was as if this was their den. More and more, that made sense to Ken. These creatures were not walking dead at all, but infected people that were changing. If there were no obvious food sources around, they would find a way to survive. This was their way, a den. He had no doubt this would make scavenging for food in the future that much more harder. Besides the obvious danger of crazy ass infected people hunting him, now they were eating the same food that the humans were after. Not only did they already have to scavenge for cans of creamed corn, but any hope of finding an unopened bag of Doritos would certainly be out of the question. Even his beloved Little Debbies would be at risk. *Not the Little Debbies!* he thought to himself as he looked up at the ceiling as if the big guy upstairs would say something like 'Don't worry, I've got you,' or something to that effect. Nothing met his gaze though.

The building was clear and not a can or box or bag of unopened food remained. If they could eat clothing, they'd have months' worth of snacks but alas, it was not to be. After the hike, the constant fear of death and the other events of the day, the trio decided to call it a night, or a morning as it were. The sun had risen to the east and bathed the building in the warm rays of the light. Using one whole rack of clothing as bedding and blankets, they created a makeshift nest for the three humans. Placing a series of knick knacks on top of a small display case on the inside of the front door that would fall if anything tried to gain entry, and blocking off the previously open window in the back room, the room was as secure as they could make it. In a perfect world, or some semblance of it, someone would stand guard. With the horrors of the day, none of the trio could keep their eyes open. Reckless or not, people did not operate without rest. They slept, tossing and turning with memories of either happiness or pain running through their weary minds. It was hard to have nightmares worse than the apocalypse, unless, of course, it was evil clowns. Clowns by themselves were scary as hell sometimes, and evil ones, all red balloons and cheap jokes would have sent anyone remaining over the edge of sanity for sure. Kenneth's dreams tended to always go back to his gaming days. Spending hours upon hours streaming his Halo and Fortnite conquests to sometimes hundreds of fans. The dreams of pulling that right trigger and seeing an enemy fall, and his kill count increase were the good ones. Generally, his brain would only entertain them for so long before it went dark, bringing up memories of horror. The worst of which was the remembrance of Billy and his mother. Seeing the life fade away from the child, and seeing the grief in his mother was the epiphany of a nightmare for him. No matter how he tried to change what happened in his nightmares, it always ended the same. The young boy dead in his arms, and his mother pulling a pistol and shooting him after a zombie attack. He startled awake, quickly pulling his gun up from under its home under a set of brand-new sweaters he had been using for warmth. It came up easily and was pointed at the door in two heartbeats. Nothing stirred as he held the weapon, watching and listening for any movement. When nothing happened, he slowly lowered the barrel.

It came to a rest beside him once again and he took in a deep breath. He slowly stood from the small pile of humanity and stretched. The two women beside him lay tangled up in each other's arms and legs. They had all slept close for warmth but there was no way he'd be caught with his arms or legs anywhere near the two as Isabel would certainly find out and he'd have to fear for his life, and no one wanted that. He walked to the back of the store, and into the small employee restroom. The water had stopped running forever ago, but that suited him just as well. He didn't need to flush for what he was doing. As he took care of business, his right hand up against the cold bare wall. His other hand ran through his long hair, causing goosebumps to ripple through him. Fun fact ladies, one of the tenderest things you can do for a man is run your hand through his hair. Unless he's bald or otherwise bare-headed, then the advice probably falls flat. He heard noise in their sleeping room and he made to make for his pistol, which he had strapped to his side. His hand stopped though as he heard a light giggle. He sighed as he knew he wouldn't be able to go back to sleep now if the ladies were up. He finished and zipped up, walking out of the restroom to find the two women still under the covers so to speak doing God knows what. *Women were a strange breed,* he thought as he went to one of the windows and peered out. The empty parking lot beyond showed no sign of any danger. Refugees wouldn't have made the trek up the steep mountain during the panic, so it made sense that the only ones up here were this pack of infected. Behind him, the women rose from their earthly beds and bounded to the restroom. He stood stoically, avoiding turning around at all costs. He was a gentleman after all, or maybe it was just the fear of his other half. Slowly, his eyes followed the edge of the lot where a small vehicle path led to a closed gate with a series of radio antennas beyond. The real test would be finding a way to reach anyone with any semblance of success. A small building sat near the gate and his eyes fixated on it. That would be their target.

Twenty minutes passed before the two women were ready and composed enough for Kenneth to sit down and converse with them. The three of them sat, each eating a package of MREs

(Meals ready to eat). The two continued to pass glances at each other, smiling as they did so. Kenneth rolled his eyes. "Let's focus on the problem at hand, okay?" he asked the two who seemed to be genuinely upset at being interrupted. Both women looked at him with a plate of annoyance with a generous side of 'who made you boss?' He held up his hands in a placating manor. "We need to figure out what the plan is unless you just want to sit here and wait for someone to come upon us," he said. "You're right," Ashmore said, the heat from her stare slowly withering away. "What do we do once we get in there?" she asked. Ken shrugged. "I'm not really sure. I've dabbled in electronics but don't know much of anything about frequencies or anything like that," he responded. He looked at Atencio. "Don't look at me, I don't know crap about that, I was a cheerleader," she said, looking down at her feet. "We'll have to play it by ear then. Once we're done eating, how about we hop to it?" he asked the two. They both nodded and continued to shovel the unappealing food down. After marshaling their trash and readying up, they moved the display case and opened the front door slowly. The wind was cold, and at an altitude of 10,600 ft. and change, it was all prevailing. Leaving the semi warm confines of the shelter and into the harsh wind served to further wake them up to complete alertness. The trio crossed the parking lot and made it to the fence. None of the group had bolt cutters, so the plan shifted to climbing the fence. Ashmore and Atencio ran back to the gift shop, and retrieved several of the sweaters from the shop. They threw those over the barbed wire on top to avoid any unnecessary cuts or punctures. The last thing that any of them wanted was tetanus, after all, there was more than enough ways to die in the world these days. That would be a really disappointing way to go. As they all made it safely to the ground on the other side, they fanned out, looking for threats. None came. Coming to the small one-room building, Kenneth used the butt of his rifle to bash the lock until it gave. Between the elements, constant cold weather and the not-so-gentle force applied by Ken, it broke much easier than anticipated. Atencio entered first, sweeping her rifle from left to right, with Ashmore coming in right behind her. Kenneth came in immediately after. The room was clear and appeared undisturbed.

A variety of computers and screens dominated the majority of the room with long dead indicator lights on a panel to the right. A small reinforced window sat dead-center in the wall to the left. Closing the door behind them, they found the place was without power, and had been probably since the beginning of the end. "Well, this is off to a good start," Atencio said, leaning up against one of the walls. "We need to go outside," Ken said, heading for the door. "Are you serious? We just got here, and it's really cold out there," she said, shaking her head in emphasis. "I'll go, you stay," he said, walking out alone into the frigid wind. He followed the exterior wall of the building and came upon his goal. A small backup generator sat in a small fence enclosure with several barrels of diesel lining the wall. He opened up the generator cap and went to one of the three barrels. Two of the three were completely empty, he pushed those two over onto their side with little effort. Coming to the third barrel, he was sure that he would be disappointed. As he rocked it back and forth, the liquid inside sloshed around loudly. Smiling, he removed a syphoning rig from his backpack, he fed it into the drum and proceeded to transfer fuel into the genny. Once it was filled to capacity, he stopped the syphon and went through the processes of starting the generator. After several attempts, it puttered to life and with an air of satisfaction about him, Ken headed to the door of the building. Movement caught his eye and he swore to himself, pulling his rifle up to his shoulder. He looked down the sights and no longer saw anything out of the ordinary. The movement was so fast, a blur really. He lowered his weapon and looked back at where they had come. Nothing was moving and nothing was out of place. *Damn, I'm tired*, he thought as he shrugged and quickly reentered the small dwelling. The women pulled their own weapons up in response to his entry. He held out his hands and they lowered them, each letting out a breath. Inside, he found the lights and displays were slowly coming to life, like an old robot after being stuck in the cold of space for a decade. Searching around, he found an operating checklist. Looking over everything and becoming as familiar with the setup as he could, he began to fidget with switches and panels, turning them off and on and seeing what the results where. Peering out of the small window, he could also see the aircraft warning lights on the antennas were blinking now. That was a great sign. If all else, it would signify to any passing aircraft that there was someone alive here. His goal, though, was to send out a signal to increase the chances of getting rescued. The lights on the inside of the building flickered and the generator coughed several times before continuing with its duty. "The fuel might be bad," Ashmore said as she watched the spectacle. "Yeah, we might not have much time," Ken said, a fresh bead of sweat rolling down his forehead. A program running on one of the old as hell computers caught his attention. After logging in with an employee's login, which was luckily provided by a previous tenant who left their login information on a small post-it note located on the display monitor. Half of an hour later, he was still no closer to sending out a signal. The towers were sending out static already but getting anything over the airways was a problem. It hit him. By turning the towers on and off, he could send an SOS. His Morse code was rusty but between the three of them, they figured it out. He entered a series of commands into the computer and watched the lights for each antenna die, and then turn back on brightly. "This might actually work," he said as he smiled to the two women. They both smiled back, high-fiving each other. The door to the room burst open as two hunters bounded in, catching the three of them wholly off-guard. Ashmore was quickest to react, pulling her sidearm and catching one of the infected in the left lung, causing it to drop. The second bolted for Ken and leapt into the air. Ken rolled to the right, just far enough for the infected to go over his head. The unfortunate part was that it landed on a series of keyboards, causing sparks, and the entire system to begin going haywire. The lights in the room flickered on and off and the hunter, electrocuted, landed on the floor in a freshly cooked manor. Outside of the door, three more running infected could be seen about to scale the fence. As Ken looked out, a dozen zombies were slowly coming from around the novelty store. He raised his rifle again, and fired into the group, now landing on their feet on their side of the fence. The lead infected's skull exploded in gore as a high caliber round caught it through the eye with an upward trajectory. The dozen by the shop turned to two dozen and the sound of the gunfire was sure to attract more from all around. "This is not cool!" Atencio shouted as she took down one more of the hunters. Ken fired a burst into the last one standing and heard a click, and his rifle stopped firing. If you've ever used a firearm, you know that click. He was out of ammunition, and dry firing. "Oh shit," he said, throwing down his backpack, searching for any remaining magazines or even loose rounds. He came up woefully short. "I'm out!" he yelled, dropping his rifle and pulling his pistol. Two magazines of 9mm was all that he had left, between the loaded pistol and the spare in the holster. The two women took the lead, with Ken taking a defense posture. He'd save his rounds for any that got too close. The two dozen zombies turned to three dozen and the parking lot was quickly filling up with walking dead. Another loud click as Atencio went dry. "I'm out too!" she shouted in frustration, spitting out a series of curses that would make a sailor blush. "This isn't going to work, we need to evac!" Ken yelled to the two. A rock cliff to one side, and dozens of undead spreading out along the fence line left their choices limited. The lights of the room and antennas behind them were still flickering wildly. Ken pointed, "Look, over there!" he shouted. The two women turned and followed his pointing. Six, no, seven of the hunters walked from side to side, just out of weapon range. They didn't advance, but instead seemed like they were patrolling the area. "They're waiting for us to try to leave or for the zombies to get in," Ken said. "I hate smart fucking zombies so much," Ashmore said, her rifle lowering to her side. She pulled the magazine and counted the rounds. She had six. Not sixty, not six hundred, just six. She could try to take out the hunters but with the ranges involved, she could miss and what good would that do? "I'm going to save the last rounds," she said, pulling her backup pistol as well. "What the hell are we going to do?" Atencio shouted. "If the zombies breach the gate, hiding in the building will do no good. They'll just overwhelm us and wait us out," Ken said. "So then, what's the plan?" Atencio asked again, fear beginning to take hold. Ken pointed to the nearest large antenna. "We go up."

Running for the nearest tower, they began to climb the ladder in place for maintenance. The wind naturally picked up and they were rocked with the ice-cold chill of high altitude. Two of the hunters saw the trio bolt and decided the wait was over. They jumped the fence in no time and began to climb up after the fresh warm meat. The zombies below pushed through the gate and made their way to the tower as well. Ken was last up and saw the infected hunter below him gaining ground fast. Stopping his climb, he fired three rounds down the ladder and directly into the tops of their heads. They fell back into their brethren below. When they felt that they had climbed high enough, they found solace in a small catwalk that circled the tower. They grouped up together, once again trying to maintain body heat. Kenneth watched as the base of the tower was completely surrounded. The remaining hunters stood at the bottom, looking up, as if deciding whether or not to go for it. In the end, they didn't budge. So, the trio sat on the small walkway and waited. For what, none of them knew. It wouldn't be long before they began to get too cold and their health would begin to seriously decline. "God, a little help please?" Ken asked the clouds above. Another gust of cold wind blew into the group and they all began to shiver. "I guess that's a no," Ken said as he inched closer to the women and hugged them tight. "What a way to go." He sighed as he stared down at the undead below and fired another round in absolute frustration. Hopefully, that shot not his last.

Chapter Twenty-Nine

"Sir, we're receiving a signal," said a technician. He was sitting before a row of computer monitor and wearing a headset. A uniformed man came abreast of him. "What is it?" the uniformed man asked the tech. "It's static sir," the tech said. "What's special about that?" Uni asked him. "It wasn't there earlier sir. We've scanned all of the signals. This one is amplified and coming from the north," he said. "Can we trace it?" Uni asked. "Yes sir, pinpointing the location now. Should I respond?" Tec asked. "I think we'll respond in our own way," Uni said as he picked up a red phone in the small communications room. Two floors above the technician sat a man behind a desk in a very comfortable chair. The phone on his desk rang and he answered. "Yes?" he asked. Listening intently, he waited until the end of the dialogue. "Send a team," was his only response as he hung up the phone and continued with his duties. In this case, a riveting game of SimCity on his PC. Four men clad in black fatigues were suited up, and heavily armed within minutes. They ascended the stairs, two at a time, heading for the exit of the compound. "Where are we heading sir?" the one at the back asked the one apparently leading. "We're going back to Albuquerque. Apparently, someone is broadcasting a signal and we're going to find out who it is," he said, as the team boarded a waiting black hawk helicopter, painted in black camouflage. "Rescue or search and destroy?" the rear asked the leader. "We'll find out when we get there, won't we?" he snapped at the soldier behind him. "Yes sir," the rear said as he boarded and buckled in, deciding to keep his mouth shut for the rest of the ride. Within moments, it was airborne and heading north with all haste available.

The trio sat, huddled together for warmth as the wind gusts continued to zap what little heat they had left. One more time, a hunter had made the attempt to scale the ladder. It too was met with a bullet to the head. The zombies below, being mindless more or less simply jockeyed for position around the tower, and reached their hands up as if they were going to somehow reach their prey. "Are we going to die?" Ashmore asked, shivering. "No, we'll be fine," Ken muttered back, trying to keep the trembling out of his own voice. "Bet?" Atencio asked. Kenneth glanced at her. "You want to bet on our survival?" he asked. "If we die, it won't matter, will it?" she retorted. "I guess not, but I bet you a case of beer that we make it out of here," Ken said. "Ew, who even likes beer?" Atencio said in disgust. "Okay, what do you have?" he asked her, turning to give her his full attention. "A case of Smirnoff Ice," she said with a grin. "Ew, are you serious?" Ken asked, giving the same tone as her previous one. "How about this, if... or when rather, we make it out of here, I will drink a case of beer and you two can get the Smirnoff," he said. The two women nodded to each other. "Deal," she said, reaching out a hand to shake his. He did not reach his own hand out to shake it. "Wow, that's rude," Atencio said, pulling her hand back. Ken's eyes still had not moved to acknowledge her. "Hello??" she said, putting her hand in front of his eyes, the fire inside of her beginning to ignite. Cold or not, she'd unleash the small woman fury that she always kept inside if he didn't start paying attention to her when she was talking to him. He finally looked down at her. "What the hell?" she asked. He stood up, and checked the ammunition in his pistol. The two women stood as well, not sure at all of what he was doing, but watching his every move. He looked up and saw them both staring at him. "It worked," he said, as he pointed out over the Albuquerque area. The brown and tan sand and adobe houses below mixed to create a collage of warm colors. The clouds had moved on from the previous day and with the sun coming directly over them, they could see the city with perfect clarity. A black object was hovering and moving over the city with a fast rate of speed. "That's our ride?" Ashmore asked, excitement and relief flowing through her. Atencio grasped her in a hug, and they jumped up and down, holding each other like only women can do. For guys, that's a no go. Sorry, that's rule 37 of the man code. Kenneth watched as the helicopter banked towards them and rose up into the air. "Ladies?" he asked, his own previous merriment disappearing with each passing moment. They didn't listen. *Why don't they ever listen?* he asked himself with frustration as he put his arms between them and separated them. "We should make ourselves as un-noticeable as possible. Like now," he told them as he proceeded to lay down on the freezing steel of the tower's catwalk. "Why in the hell would we do that when we're about to be rescued?" Atencio asked, a bit of peevishness coming through in her tone. "Probably because that's not one of our helicopters. Get down. Now!" he told her, his eyes conveying in no uncertain terms that he was dead serious. The women looked at the incoming helicopter, painted jet-black heading straight for them. "Well, grab my ears while you fuck me in the butt," she said as she too lay down. Ken stared at her, in absolute confusion. "Calm down, it's just a saying," she told him as Ashmore lay next to them. "How the Jesus and his salted crackers is that a saying?" he asked, his voice quieting substantially. "It's like when someone says, 'well, fuck me' when something goes wrong. It's like that but way better," she said matter of factly. "Whatever, that's weird.

Damned kids and their damned stupid sayings. Let's pretend to be dead now. They're here."

The helicopter passed overhead quickly, making an observation pass, and then banking quickly to the right. It came back around, making a second pass, this time, much slower. As it came around for a third, it had slowed down immensely and eventually came to a steady hover over the empty parking lot. Two black ropes fell from either side of the bird and four men rappelled down to the pavement. With weapons at the ready, they immediately began firing into the group of undead at the base of the tower with unrelenting high caliber firepower. As the zombies turned to face the new enemy, they marched in unison towards the new food. The remaining hunters though, somehow saw the writing on the wall and booked it in the opposite direction, and out of the line of sight of the newcomers. It only took a few minutes for the rifle rounds of the four men to completely destroy the mob of undead. As the last bullet left the barrel, the trio on the tower had not moved. Their eyes though had tracked all of the action, but they wanted to seem as close to shadows as physically possible. As the still smoking barrels of the men below searched for targets and came up short, they lowered. The four men advanced, with the helicopter still hovering above in a holding pattern. Watching their corners, they entered the radio building. The generator was still running, and the lights were still flickering on and off. They quickly pulled out of the building and cleared the rest of the fenced off area. One of the men in black walked back to the destroyed fence gate, and looked around. The other three fell in behind him, taking up defense positions. The curious one looked back at the tower, seeing the previously killed bodies of the infected at the base of the structure. His eyes followed the length of the ladder up, when they finally came to a rest on the trio, still unmoving. "Shit." Ken sighed as he watched the events unfold. The four men walked to the base of the tower and watched the three. "Hello up there!" one man shouted, with an Australian accent. They didn't respond. "We know you're still alive mates, the generator is still on, and these bodies are fresh," he shouted up, pointing back at the building, then at the hunters' dead by their feet. "What do we do?" Ashmore asked quietly. "Stay put," Ken whispered. "If we have to come up there to get you, we're going to have some problems," another man said, with a deep southern drawl. A thin man whispered to the rest. "We don't have time for this," he said. "Fire a shot," the southern man said in response. The thin man raised his rifle and fired one round. It ricocheted off of the metal and into Atencio's leg. She screamed in pain, clutching her wound. "I said fire a round, not hit them, you dumbass!" the southern man turned and laid into the thin man, who withered under his administrations. Ken stood up, and bent over the now bleeding Atencio and withdrew a medical kit from his small backpack. Slowly wrapping the wound, he made sure that it was a tight fit. The round had grazed her just enough to bleed. It would hurt her to walk but she'd live, or so he hoped. "How about y'all come down now, so no one else gets hurt?" the southern man yelled to the trio, while eying the thin man in the rear guard. "Go ahead. We've played our cards." Ken said, nodding to Ashmore. She nodded back and began to descend the ladder. He had Atencio go next, and he went last. As his feet hit the ground, he was immediately thrown back against the ladder as he was searched. His pistol and all of his ammunition were stripped away. His knife and even his multi tool were pulled out and flung a short distance away into a pile of like gear from the two women. He then was placed on his knees, facing the men with his hands on his head.

"Who are you?" the southern man asked. Ken's guess was that this man was definitely the leader. "Who are you?" Ken responded with his own question. The southern nodded to one of the men who then, not so gently, placed his first into Ken's gut. He hit the ground hard, feeling the wind vacate his body. He sucked in breath with small raspy gasps as he tried his best to recover the life-giving air. "I'll ask the questions. Y'hear?" he asked, eyeing the two women. They both nodded. "Who are you?" he asked again, looking at Ashmore and Atencio for an answer. They both kept silent. The man who threw the punch walked to Atencio, and pressed down hard onto her bandaged wound. She screamed in agony as he squeezed the fresh bullet wound. "Stop!" Ashmore yelled, and the man did stop. He turned to look at her. "Please, stop," she said, tears falling freely from her eyes. "We were looking for survivors," she said as the man let go of Atencio and stood straight up, motioning for Ashmore to continue. "What are you doing out in the middle of nowhere?" he asked. "We were being chased. We got cornered," she said, a fresh bout of sobs sweeping over her. The man looked at her with disgust. "That gear isn't civilian," he said, pointing to their empty rifles laying in the pile of equipment. "Neither are those fatigues," he said, pointing to her outfit. The camo tops and pants lending credence to what the man was saying. "Cannon AFB," she said simply. He nodded. "The truth will set you free," the southern man said from his spot with a grin. He motioned to the waiting chopper, which then proceeded to land in the parking lot. As its engine slowly shut off, the sound of the silence swept over the crest. "I'm in a bit of a pickle," the man said, scratching his nonexistent beard. "I'm sure that my superiors would love to have a chat with y'all. Especially considering where you're coming from," he said. Ken had finally righted himself and sat, once again, on his knees. He proceeded to stare at the men with unfiltered hatred. "I don't like you though, and we tend to kill things we don't like," he said, as if it were completely normal. "Especially you," he said, pointing to Ken, who only seemed to snarl in response. "I think we could have a bit of fun first before we take some of you back," he said with a smile. Whatever military bearing the man had once had, it was obvious that it was gone now. He was a stone-cold killer, and probably more. "You gonna make us squeal like a pig?" Ken asked the man, looking into his eyes. The man met his gaze. "I was thinking about it, yeah," he smiled back. The women looked at each other, fresh fear evident on their faces. "I'm privy to the athletic lookin' one myself," said the southern. "I think we should get to know each other before we go on our merry way back. I never seemed to have much luck with women like you before the shit hit the fan. I figure this is my sign that it's time, if you know what I mean," he said, lifting his rifle, pointing it at Ashmore. She was pale with fear, and didn't move a muscle. "Get up, and go over yonder," he said, waving his rifle in his intended direction. She still didn't move. He brought the barrel closer until it was right up against her forehead. She stared up at him, visibly shaking. "I'd hate to splat your pretty head all over the place. Let's go," he said, pointing at the radio shack. She stood, and began to walk to the building. Not three footsteps had been taken before the two were stopped in their tracks. "No!" a shout from behind the southern man broke the silence. He turned to see Atencio on her feet and heading straight for him, a knife previously concealed in her bra raised high. She reached him just as the sound of a rifle firing one shot filled the air. She took the impact in her back, and fell forward. The knife fell, missing his heart, but with a downward trajectory. The blade cut deep into his larger than normal post apocalypse gut, and immediately blood began to pour from the man. Atencio hit the gravel face first. Ashmore was there in a heartbeat, holding her head in her arms. "Baby, no no no," she repeated as she cradled her head into her arms. Blood drained out of her wound and quickly drenched the back of her military fatigues. Atencio lay, unmoving; the bullet having separating two of her invertebrates, paralyzing her. Her eyes met Ashmore as she continued to bleed, and as everyone around them looked on. "I love you," Atencio said, a ghost of a smile creeping over her face. "I love you too. I need you. Stay with me. Please babe, you'll be okay," Ashmore whispered to her, trying to force her will into her body. Their eyes stared into each other's, words and emotions being sent back and forth without needing to be spoken at all. The bond that had formed between them acting as a bridge. Slowly, Atencio's eyes fluttered and closed. She tried to fight it, of that there was no doubt. Fighting was what she knew. The light from the end of the tunnel became too much to deny. In the brightness of the white light before her eyes, she saw her family. Her mother and father, standing before her, becoming her onward with welcoming smiles. The feeling of warmness and the loss of the earthly feelings of pain slowly left her. As the light grasped hold of her as she let out her last breath, her only regret of not doing enough to protect Ashmore fading away into nothingness as she left this plane of existence. "No, no, no!" Ashmore shouted, rocking back and forth, "Wake up, wake up," she told her lover. It was useless. The girl, the fiery soldier, the caring friend, and the love of her life was dead. "The bitch cut me," the leader said, as another man in black put pressure on the wound. The words, cutting through the silence around Ashmore. "I'm gonna have a good ole time cutting you two up," he said as he looked down at the now dead woman. "Pity. She was gorgeous. She would have made a lot of men back at base very happy," he said with a grin. Ashmore pulled her head up and stared at him. Her eyes were filled with menace and hate and sorrow. It was enough to make him take a step back. "Let's get them bagged and tagged and back to HQ so I can get cleaned up," he said. Two of the men in black lifted Ashmore and Kenneth up off of the ground and began to move them towards the helicopter. "No! I can't leave her!" Ashmore yelled as she fought the man holding her. They were going to leave her friend there, like a bunch of common trash. She punched and kicked at her captors but to no avail. The man was simply stronger and faster than she was. As they neared the helicopter, a series of events played out. Life has a way of linking random events together into a term that we use all too freely; coincidence. To some, the word is meaningless as there may be no such thing. In this case though, and through Ken's eyes, it was the case. The rotors of the bird began to start up, the engine once again returning to life. A whoosh and a massive explosion erupted, its concussion knocking all of the participants to the ground. The jet black helicopter quickly became a smoldering burning wreck with smaller secondary explosions erupting inside of the now hunk of scrap. "What the fuck?" the southern yelled as he picked himself up. Two United States Air Force black hawk helicopters came into view from the east. The trails of the missile that had been fired, led straight to one of the two choppers. As the soldiers and the captives below watched, the two helicopters took up positions around the group. Both aircraft were fully armed with missiles and door gunners, all of which were aimed squarely at the men clad in black below. "Drop your weapons immediately, or we will fire on you," a woman's voice announced from the leading helicopter's loudspeakers. "Do it," the southern said, as they all laid their rifles on the ground. Knowing that they could fire at the choppers above, but short of using rockets, it would be an almost useless gesture, he stood and looked on, defeated. "One by one, you will approach this helicopter. Keep your hands on your head, and walk in a single file line. Any attempts to retrieve a weapon will result in being fired upon," the loud woman said again. The black fatigued men did as they were told. The last of the four, the southern looked back at Ashmore. "I could have been your daddy," he said with a smile. She met his gaze and walked to the discarded gear. Quickly finding what she was looking for, her hands grasping her Ruger 9mm pistol, she turned and shot him almost point blank in the head. The bullet exploded out the back of his skull, brain matter and skull fragments raining down behind him as he fell backwards. "Put it down!" the woman's voice from the helicopter yelled out. Ashmore did as she was told and dropped it back to the ground. She turned and attempted to pick up Atencio's body. Struggling, Kenneth walked over and hefted up the petite woman. For him, she was extremely light, unbelievably so. The weight of her death though would weigh on all of them heavily for the rest of their lives. The sarcastic, quick witted, fun loving girl was now just another casualty in man's war with man. Together, they hefted her up into the waiting helicopter. All of their gear was left in the pile, along with the soldiers' rifles as the helicopters raised into the air and barreled back towards their destination. Cannon Air Force Base.

Chapter Thirty

The two Air Force black hawk helicopters landed with no further issue. An assortment of base personnel met them at the tarmac. From heavily armed MPs to doctors and mechanics. As Ken and Ashmore disembarked, they saw Jaylin, Rachel and Isabel waiting for them. Isabel immediately ran for Kenneth, hoping to scoop him up in her arms and never let him go. Her pace slowed as she saw his eyes meet hers. He turned around though, their eye contact only brief enough for her to see pain in those deep brown eyes. Her run became a walk and then she stopped entirely as she watched Ken and Ashmore pull the lifeless body of her friend from inside of the helicopter. Isabel's hand went immediately to her mouth and tears began to fall like a pipeline coming straight from her heart as she realized what was going on. Jaylin and Rachel behind her were in shock as well, watching the events unfold. A medical team was immediately at the helicopter and loaded Atencio onto a stretcher. Ashmore was pushed back, away from her dead friend. The team took her, directly to the ad hock hospital and left Ken and Ashmore behind. The numbness of the events of the past few days veiled whatever happiness they had hoped to have upon arrival home. Six military police officers, heavily armed reached the helicopter and began to escort the four black clad men to waiting holding cells. Ken and Ashmore watched them leave, as they too were ushered forward in another direction and into the medical wing. Mandatory checkups were all that they could expect for the next few hours. It wasn't the homecoming for them that anyone had ever expected. Isabel was swept up in arms alright, but it was not Ken's. It was Rachel and Jaylin who huddled together with her, their tears cascading down like a waterfall of epic proportions.

As was a newly-founded tradition, the base held a memorial service, required for any base personnel or civilians that perished after the fall. Each human life was significant and each loss of one was a tragedy. The base brass and civilian council understood this. Work detail came to a halt and anyone who knew Atencio was present for the ceremony. A graveyard had been constructed outside of the base to the south, with already over a hundred crosses handmade with names stenciled into them. A fresh grave was dug for Atencio, with her casket being made out of simple 2x4's which the base managed to find in good supply. The wood was cut and patched together to make a deathbed that pre fall would have fetched a very inexpensive price, if any at all. Considering that the entire world had fallen apart though, it was the best that they could do. As storm clouds reached the base, a preacher spoke about the turmoil of life and death and as they walk through the valley of death, they shall fear no evil. Ashmore tuned that out, as she stared at her dead lover. It was not until Kenneth, freshly released from medical spoke up. "Alyssa was what many of us would consider a great friend. Someone who while she'd complain about damn near anything, would always come through for us. She was a kind soul and had, in the end, sacrificed herself for people that she loved. She saved many lives, and had helped to make this place what it is today. The world is darker without her rays of sarcastic sunshine. She will be truly missed," he said, grabbing a shovel to his right. The 21-gun salute rang out into the silence of the day, the crowd around the casket stood and watched quietly and respectfully. Taps began to play, the song long played in honor of fallen heroes encompassing everyone's souls as they stood as it began to sprinkle and the clouds began to unleash their own tears onto the earth. Ashmore stayed stock-still, refusing to move a muscle as she watched her closest friends begin to bury the small petite woman with whom she had spent many adventures with. The one who had helped her out of her darkest place after she had lost all that was dear to her. As the coffin below was covered with dirt, she felt a part of herself being buried with her. Many in the crowd looked on, watching her, rather than the actions being taken by the burial detail. As the last of the pile was moved onto the grave, and people began to move away, back to their duties, she stood like a statue in a park, staring down. Many minutes later, Ken touched her shoulder. She, at first, tried to shrug it off, but he came around full speed and hugged her with all of the strength that he had. At first, she was stiff and refused to truly feel the embrace. Like a germophobe being touched by someone with a cold, she resisted it with all of her being. People though are not slaves to their own mind; they tend to be slaves to their heart. As this strong man, her dear friend held her, the dam broke. The flood of sobs erupted like Mount Vesuvius. The pain rocked her like nothing else had in her entire life. Even the death of her family had not felt this soul wrenching. Maybe it was that she had almost nothing left until she had nothing. Ken held her for what seemed like hours and she let out every ounce of water left in her system. Coming up dry, she whispered a "thank you" to Ken as she turned and headed back towards the residential area. The sorrow and pain that she felt flow through her quickly turned to anger as she took step after step. Lightning and thunder erupted overhead as she swore that she would get her revenge. Ashmore and Ken too would be joining the raid. Ashmore would not let those responsible get away with it. Not if she could help it.

The following morning, the small group of friends met at the dining hall. Quietly, they ate, and spoke short bouts to one another, but each of them was reserved. It was the calm before the storm and they all knew it. That night, they would be raiding the compound. The transport helicopters being used for the mission were kept under doubled 24-hour armed guard. They were taking no chances with more sabotage. The mission was a need-to-know, and a large majority of the base simply did not need to know. That left their discussion about the upcoming mission hushed and muted whenever anyone else walked by. It might have been comical to see the group become silenced each and every time someone passed behind them while they ate, and would no doubt raise some eyebrows and peak some curiosity. It didn't matter though. In twelve hours' time, they'd be on the move, and no one short of God and all of His angels could stop them from getting their revenge on the assholes responsible for so many deaths around them. It was time to get a piece of their attackers, and they were ready for it.

Several hours later, hundreds of miles away and deep underground; an infected man made its move. For the unfortunate medical tech who happened to pass by and hear racket come inside of a holding cell, it would be his final mistake. The infected waited for the man to open the door before pulling the tech into the room, biting deeply into its corroded artery. The man's screams were quickly silenced as his life fluid drained in mass amounts. He slowly fell to the floor with the infected holding onto him tight, like a leech to a river swimmer's foot. Once the blood stopped pumping, the rather intelligent infected pulled the keycard name tag off of the corpse and swiped it against the reader. It took only four tries for the light on the pad to turn green and the door to unlock with a light click. The smarty pants slowly entered the hall, and began to swipe the keycard again and again against every keypad that it came across as it roamed the halls. Each door opened, with more infected filling the halls behind it. Their time had finally come.

Two hallways from the loose infected, Shepherd lay, his restraints still in place, and the machine continuously pumping serum 128 into his left arm. While he himself was unconscious, the virus within him was not. The constant supply of infection had overwhelmed his body's defenses. His mind and some could say even his soul were on the run, and the Z bug would not miss the opportunity to spread. Possessed by the entity attacking him, his head turned slightly as the sound of commotion from down the hallway caught his attention. A minute or two later, the keypad for his room lit up green and opened. The smarty pants infected entered, with fresh blood dripping from its mouth. It looked at Shep curiously, and walked to the bed. Shepherd watched the infected approach with grey, almost black lifeless eyes. The smarty sniffed at the man below it as it decided to take a bite or not. Zombies, or even the living infected had an unquenchable appetite after all. A snack served on a silver platter would be greatly appreciated, any time, day or night. Its facial expression soon turned to confusion as it looked into the restrained man's eyes. They stared at each other for what seemed like an eternity.

Shepherd looked down at his restraints, and smarty slowly pulled on the wrist bands until they became loose and opened, releasing Shepherd's right arm. His left arm and then his feet were eventually free. Shepherd stood, with smarty watching his every move. The man he used to be was nowhere to be found as he stared at the mirror on the opposite side of the room. Shepherd grinned, a dark humorless smile reaching across his face as he walked to the mirror. Placing two hands against the glass, his smile changed to a growl as he followed smarty out of the room and into the chaos beginning across the compound.

Inside the observation room, just on the other side of the mirror, stood Sydney. Trembling, with a hand over her mouth in horror, she watched her prized test subject being unleashed onto the world right before her eyes. *This can't be happening*, she repeated in her head as she watched the scene unfold before her eyes. The keypad to her right beeped green. She turned slowly, feeling increasing terror rise within her. A figure entered the room, and gently let the door close behind it. Although darker than the cell in the observation room, it was still bright enough to see with perfect clarity who it was. Shepherd stood before her; his grin plastered on his face. His grey eyes watched her every move. "It's not my fault. They made me…" she started. His grin fell away and he slammed the glass with his fist, causing a crack in the mirror. Her mouth immediately slammed shut and she backed away from the man, no, the creature before her. Every step that she took backwards, he took one forward. Her back came to rest against the cold concrete of the wall behind her. "I can make you better," she said, trying a different approach. He tilted his head slightly, like a dog would do when hearing a strange noise. "Yes, I can make you better. Just let me go, and I'll make it happen." He took another step, until they were almost nose to nose. His breath was warm, with a hint of a smell of something that she could not place. She shook with fear, sweat and tears falling in rivulets. She turned her head as he brought his head near her, sniffing her ear, and then her neck. "I do like you, they made me pretend… I..." her sentence was cut off as he sunk his teeth deep into her neck, and held her tight as she struggled. The previously wonderful breasts pressing against him once again, only to be the last time. She punched him again and again, trying to get free but he held on tight, like a dog in a fight for its life. She slowly began to lose consciousness and fell into him, her body shaking. He ripped upward, pulling tendon and meat upwards as he did so. Sprays of blood splattered the glass like a shower curtain in an old horror movie. Shepherd took his time with her, much more time than was necessary. The elation at having ended her life in return for the pain she had caused him helping to spur him on. Several hours he spent in that observation room, savoring every single bloody moment of it.

Chapter Thirty-One

The raiding party took off shortly before sunset, with the goal of giving the outpost as little opportunity for noticing them as possible. The group had strict radio silence, and flew by night vision. The pilots were trained for this, but most of the passengers were not. Nearly riding the dirt at some points, they flew low, much to the chagrin of the passengers. Rachel held on for dear life, harkening back to the time when her own helicopter had gone down over the desert and depositing her right into enemy territory. That whole trip could have ended far worse for her than it did. If it hadn't been for Shepherd's shenanigans, and his rescue, she had no doubt she would have met some horrible fate. That thought led her to think about him once again. The man who stole her heart. It felt like such a long time since she had seen him. Her fiancé, the man who always seemed to have a witty, sarcastic answer for anything. The man who steer any conversation towards sex in the most awkward and hilarious ways. The memories of their previous home at the apartment complex in downtown Albuquerque, the onslaught that forced them from that home and led them to Cannon AFB. The times they sat together and told each other about their favorite memories. The time Shepherd had told her when he slipped on a treadmill at a gym due to him forgetting to double-knot his shoes, and how scraped up his knee was. That had made her laugh out loud. She had seen him run and could picture it completely. Sure enough, he still forgot to double-knot his shoes, even after that event. The time when he walked around his store in a blow-up dinosaur costume just to hand out candy to kids on Halloween. All of the crazy stories that he shared about working in retail. Don't let anyone tell you that retail is easy. From stories of thieves sticking sub sandwiches and wine down their pants to the time he had to hogtie someone who kept trying to fight him while waiting for the police to show up, and the time someone brought a bucket of human feces and dumped it into a toilet in the women's room, requiring him to use a dustpan to shovel it into a second toilet just to get the first one to flush. Rachel smiled at that. He would do everything needed and more. He was a provider, a giver, and she missed him. She missed him so much. The tears that always seemed to be just under the surface made their appearance and she tried with all of her might to push them back deep down. A single tear fell from her right eye and she quickly wiped it away. He was most likely dead now, somewhere in the middle of nowhere. Out of fear, out of concern for the others in her party, she left him. She had abandoned him. She felt that to her soul and knew it would be a skeleton in her closest for the rest of her life. She should have gone back, should have said fuck off to the others and looked for him. She shook her head to clear her mind, not wanting to go down that road once again. She would wear the ring that he had given her until the end of time. They hadn't been married; she knew. That did not change the fact that she had felt as if their souls were intertwined. That they were meant to be. As her fingers moved the ring back and forth on her finger, she stared out over the expanse of the New Mexico desert. The occasional barren tree or cactus rushing by outside of the open door. Not a light could be seen anywhere in the distance. The miles swept by as she stared out the door, her hair being tossed around every which way as the wind tore through the crew area.

She snapped out of her gaze just as they entered line of sight of the compound. The pilots passed the word on that they were almost at their destination. One minute until they'd disembark and seek vengeance on the wrong doers of the world. That was the way Rachel saw it. She was ready to get back at those that had caused them all so much grief. The four black hawk helicopters slowed with a tilt of the front of the aircrafts upwards. The movement caught Rachel off-guard, and she felt slightly nauseous. The aircraft evened out, and then plummeted almost straight down towards the earth. It landed with a thunk, and a "Go go go!" was shouted from all around the inside of the bird. Everyone piled out, rifles at the ready. Besides a simple and ordinary chain link fence, she saw nothing that resembled a base of any kind. A small concrete entrance sat alone with a single metal door barring their way. No lock on the exterior of the door was present. Natalie and Cassandra took the lead, smashed the door inwards in just a moment, and led the way down the stairs and into the facility. As they entered the stairwell, they heard the unmistakable sound of an alarm. The blaring noise was louder the lower that they got. "They know we're here," Sergeant Emsley whispered as she stood behind the two air guardsmen. They filed down the stairs, with other squads behind them on the upper levels following them down. They came to a guard post and a much heavier steel door. The door was locked, with no one visible through the small window. Cassandra and Natalie began placing charges along the hinges of the door. The group took cover as the two women stood a ways back and grinned at each other while Natalie pushed the button on the detonator. The door exploded, with shards of metal flying in every direction. One of the pieces just barely missing Cassandra. She ducked as it clanged against the stairs to her right. She stood and smiled. "Well, butter my butt and call me a biscuit, that was close." Natalie fist bumped her with a laugh and they made their way forward. The guard post was completely void of guards. That, in itself, was odd enough. The flashing red lights lit the hallway past the line of desks and lockers. Several rifles were missing from opened cages lining one wall. Camera feeds showed on several monitors of the outside perimeter, which still showed men and women filing down the stairs. "What the hell?" Elmsley said as she looked over the room. "I guess we don't have a welcome party," Isabel said quietly. Rachel nodded as she too looked on. Slowly, the group continued down a narrow concrete hallway. Blood coated the right wall, and a corpse of a heavily armed soldier lying flat on the floor. Elmsley held up her hand, signaling everyone to hold up. She approached the body and looked it over. Multiple bites were evident, with large chunks of meat missing from his exposed arms and legs, and neck. "Infected," she said, loud enough to get the point across to the group. She pulled out a large combat knife and stabbed it into the eye of the corpse, making sure to twist it around to scramble as much of the brain as possible. This one would not turn. She pulled the knife free and wiped it on the corpse's camo shirt. She then stood and motioned for the team to follow. They entered another stairwell, and then another hallway that guided them to a split hallway. On the right was a sign that said simply, 'Hanger' and another that said 'Receiving.' Elmsley pointed both directions, and two small squads entered each of those hallways as the main group continued downwards. She heard gunshots from the groups above and one by one, they responded to her radio calls with muffled "Clears." Those teams would roll through those assigned rooms and then follow the main group back downwards once any hostiles were taken care of. The lead group continued downwards and soon arrived at another juncture. This one read 'Housing' and 'Medical.' Corpses by the dozen littered the hallway leading out of the housing wing. The main group then split into two more groups, one sweeping the medical wing and one the housing. The housing group immediately met with resistance and began to fire into a small group of infected huddled over the body of a petite woman, as they pushed each other aside to get at whatever fresh meat that they could. The pop pop pop of rifle rounds could be heard by the medical group as they began to clear room after room. Each room that they came to was unlocked. In four rooms, they found nearly completely devoured corpses. All four had been in the same area, Section C as it was listed on the 'you are here' display. One of the last rooms in the wing caught Rachel's attention. The door was unlocked, like all of the rest. As she entered, moving her rifle from left to right as she and two others cleared it, she felt something. She couldn't describe it, had she been pressed to. She felt a familiar presence in the air. A machine with a large batch of black liquid sat alongside a soiled hospital bed. Restraints sat wide open, with a clipboard still attached to the front of the bed. She approached it curiously, and pulled it from its hook. A wide assortment of notes was scrabbled all over the sheets. She could not tell what a majority of them meant. It wasn't until four pages down, she saw photo. A photo of someone that she recognized. Shepherd. "Oh my God," she whispered to herself as she read what was written.

"The subject seems to be in a comatose state. Serum 128 shows great promise as it has continuously kept an otherwise immune individual in somewhat of a stalemate. The body can be described as near-death, but whether the virus is not strong enough to take full control, or the host is strong enough to hold off the infection is yet to be determined. Further experimentation required," it said. Another note was written on the lower right-hand side of the chart. "Increase dosage request approved," with a date scribbled under it. Yesterday. The dosage was increased just one day ago. Rachel held her hand to her mouth, feeling the guilt and the pain returning, only to have it turn to an insane amount of worry. He was still alive, and he was here. She retrieved her radio and spoke quickly. "All personnel please be on the lookout for a Caucasian male, 6'1, brown eyes, a short beard and brown hair. Individual is a member of Cannon AFB and has been kept here as a prisoner," she finished. She turned to the two others in the room, and went to leave in a hurry. She stopped as her eyes, once again, came across the machine next to the bed. She re-entered the room, and removed the canister from the machine, placing it snugly into her utility backpack. She nodded to the two and they left. They entered the next unlocked door and came to the room on the other side of the mirror. There, what was left of a corpse of a woman lay shredded on the bare tile floor. The only reason they knew it was a woman was by the full head of hair left behind on top of the pile of leftover meat and tendons and shining white bone. "Jesus H Christ," one of the soldiers with her said as he immediately turned to his right and puked, adding that smell to the smell of the canned woman. That thought almost sent Rachel over the edge too. She looked down, and traced the floor with her flashlight. Sure enough, footprints led from the pile, out the door and into the hall. She followed the steps and sure as shit realized that she had missed the footprints on their way through the hall. The prints eventually faded into another staircase leading down. Two other teams had been instructed to move on ahead of them downwards. As Rachel once again neared the stairs, gunshots were prevalent from down the steps. Maybe it was curiosity, bravado, or something else, but she continued down, the rifle shots getting louder with each step. As she neared the next floor, they were met by the backs of both squads, firing into a hallway with signs showing a conference room and offices. Dozens of infected, some no doubt having been previously tenants of the facility here, still in the black fatigues or lab coats and even a secretary or two. Seeing an infected trying to walk in high heels would have been absolutely hilarious to Rachel had the radio not caught her attention. "We found him," someone said. She stopped in her tracks. With the screams of men and women around her, the rounds flying and the smell of gunpowder in the hair, she stood stock-still. She reached for her radio and spoke. "Is he okay?!" she almost yelled in the heat of the moment. It was Jaylin who replied her. "I'm sorry. He's gone." Rachel heard the woman, her friend say back to her in the softest voice she had ever heard her use. Her entire world came crashing down around her. She slowly slid her back along the right wall, the people ahead of her still trying to push forward. The two soldiers that had previously been with her moved up to help, adding their own fire to the line. Rachel though, was lost. "Are you sure?" she almost whispered into the radio. "See for yourself," Jaylin said.

Chapter Thirty-Two

Jaylin and Isabel had continued on with Elmsley and others, fighting their way forward in the infected facility. The hope of completely clearing it seemed to be more and more a farfetched idea. They were sending hundreds of rounds towards infected that seemed to crawl in and out of crevices like cockroaches on the kitchen floor when the light gets turned on. These infected were stubborn and sneaky with several soldiers meeting their untimely demise by walking by supposedly cleared rooms only to be dragged into the waiting mouth of yet another infected. Oddly, there were very few undead zombies. Almost all of the infected encountered were of the fresh and fast variety. It didn't really matter to either of the women though, they had a job to do and that job was to destroy all of them with absolutely no fucks given. They reached a laboratory of some kind, with medical equipment shoved into every possible inch with only enough room for two people to walk side by side along the entire room. Isabel fired again as two runners leapt up from below a table and headed straight for them. The first one caught the brunt of the ammunition as the three round burst nearly split it in half. The second one landed on the floor in front of the two women, and proceeded to smash headlong into the two. Both women went sprawling, and even Elmsley who had been not far behind was taken aback. She raised her own weapon to fire, but she couldn't risk it without hitting the two women. The infected woman with greying hair, in a business suit reached the other side of the two, snarled as it looked back at them before attempting to continue forward and up the stairs, it was heading right for Elmsley. She had a clear shot and she took it. She dispatched it with two quick semi-automatic shots. The thing went down just inches away from her black steel toed boots. Jaylin helped Isabel up, looking back at Elmsly. "It was trying to run away," Isabel said aloud. Jaylin nodded gravely. "That's not a good sign at all." Elmsly nodded as she fired another round into the head at point blank range just to make sure they'd have no further issues with that one. "Let's move," Elmsley said as she took point. They continued through the tight confines of the laboratory, checking under each table slowly and methodically. A room at the end of the lab had a door ajar, and as Elmsley stopped to read over a clipboard on a table to the right, Jaylin peered in curiously. The door had a glass window inserted in the high center of it, and in the middle of the room, with a syringe in hand, stood Shepherd. Beside him stood an infected who seemed intrigued by his every move. Jaylin and Isabel rifles both rose up to meet the threat. Both figures turned to stare at them. Jaylin took it all in. On a table were over a dozen vials of black liquid, each one labeled with a different serial number. The one in Shepherds hand, read Serum 129 with a skull and bones warning attached. The women watched as neither of the figures made a move towards them. Shepherd had turned towards them, but his flat eyes stared blankly at them. His shirt was stained with fresh and old blood, with his mouth still red from the previous feedings. His hands had not stopped moving though as he plunged the needle into a blackened vein in his arm.

He pushed the plunger forward, the liquid quickly entering his body. He let out a groan and his eyes rolled back into his head. After a moment, he dropped the syringe and his eyes came back to focus on the two women. The two women watched in horror as it all unfolded. Elmsley had apparently finished her reading and entered, trying to see what the two were staring at. Within a heartbeat, she pulled her rifle up and fired. Shepherd moved unnaturally quick to his right, ducking behind a table and the infected that had been at his side went for the three women. Jaylin pulled the door closed just as the gnashing teeth of the infected hit the window to the room. She locked the door from the outside and watched in disgust as the infected tried to force its way out, bashing its hands and its head against the glass. The door held firm. After a minute of attempting, it backed away slowly. Shepherd stood back up and walked to the door. Calmly trying the door handle, and finding it locked, he peered back at the two with grey, unforgiving eyes. It watched them for another few moments before turning back and continuing with what he had been doing before they arrived. A suitcase stood on the floor near the table.

The man creature slowly took each vial and placed them each delicately into the padded suitcase as the women watched in amazement. "What the fuck was that?" Elmsley asked the two women, fear evident in her voice. "That was Shepherd."

Rachel made her way to the lab, the firefight still raging behind her. The troops were holding their own but were suffering losses that they could ill afford. If things did not improve, they'd be forced to pull out. Intel or not and captives or not, it was not worth the loss of life during an apocalypse. She walked along the darkened hallway, stepping over the first infected without a single glance. She stepped over the second with ease as well. The reality of the situation did not fully reveal itself until she found the three women still huddled around the door. Rachel approached, which startled all three of them as they all went for their weapons. She held out her hands as she approached and they let the weapons fall back into their slings. Jaylin ran to Rachel and hugged her tightly, whispering an "I'm so sorry." As she did. Rachel pushed her aside, the adrenaline spiking as she came to the door. Inside, she saw Shep. Her lover, her friend, mentor and fiancé. His back was to them and the infected inside with him stood watching the women through the glass. It made some kind of a noise that seemed to draw the attention of Shepherd. His head tilted and he slowly turned to the window... Her eyes traced his shirt, seeing the blood and the gore that had seeped into it. She thought she even saw a human ear holding onto the shirt by some mythical means. They moved up to the blood-covered neck and beard. The same beard she would stroke lovingly as they laid in bed and spoke for hours. The one that would tickle her as he'd come behind her and kiss her neck, always causing her to giggle and get goosebumps. The lips she'd kissed a million times, the nose and then, the eyes. The eyes. The brown, caring eyes of her love was gone, replaced by black pupils surrounded by a sea of grey. The eyes were focused on her, she knew, as was hers on his. It was her worst fear come true. It was at that moment that Rachel lost her mind.

The evacuation from the base was a blur, she registered the sailor Jewel giving commands from his radio. "Eagles nest, this is Eaglet One. Facility is compromised. Requesting immediate firing of the base." She was no longer cognizant of the world around her. She felt hands heft her up, and felt herself moving. "Eaglet One, this is Eagles Nest, fire mission approved. Hammer of the Gods is en route. ETA 2 hours." She heard as she felt the up and down of being carried up steep steps. Voices around her gave warning that infected were filling in behind them, and were also attempting to bar their escape from the base. The infected below continued pushing the troops up the stairwells. Precious minutes ticked by as the soldiers rained hell downwards towards the creatures below but for every one that went down, it seemed like two took their places. Eventually, they punched through the infected at the top and she felt her head hit the doorway of the guard post as she was carried out. Her body limp with uncaring. Rachel was deposited inside of a waiting black hawk as the rest of the crew filed in around her. Around her, other squads were being picked up and helicopters were lit up like Christmas trees. "Eagles nest to Eaglet One. Danger close expected in five minutes," the radio squawked. "Acknowledged," Jewel said as their helicopter rose slowly into the air. The infected fanned out of the door below and tried to latch on to any helicopter remaining. Two soldiers were pulled out of black hawks still attempting to gain altitude and were dog-piled on by a dozen infected. They rose and she moved her head involuntarily. The helicopter continued to rise and her eyes fell to the door of the facility. There, two figures stood just outside of the door, silhouetted by the lights of the hallway behind. The two figures stared onwards, watching the helicopters above. Rachel's eyes narrowed as she tried to focus on the two. The dawn of realization reached her, a moment before the first cruise missile impacted the ground behind the door. It was Shepherd, holding the black briefcase. He was loose. *How did he…* Her thoughts were cut off as a series of missiles landed around them, and the black hawks continued to bank away from the hellfire. Smoke from the explosions filled the area and she lost sight just as another one landed dead center on where she guessed the door of the base was below. The light from the hallway was erased as steel and Infected bodies were flung in every direction, some of them on fire as they lit up the night like macabre streamers. Three more explosions rocked the blast area as the black hawks moved away in the direction of Cannon AFB, to return victorious in the survivors' minds. All of them except Rachel's, Ken's, Isabel's, and Jaylin's. To them, they lost something worth far more than a victory. They lost their friend that they'd never get back. Or would they?

Epilogue

Not thirty minutes before the arrival of the Cannon AFB raiding party, a small convoy of three vehicles drove away from the facility. The Praetor sat in the rear of a black bulletproof limousine, with a comfortable leather interior and a full bar. With their running lights off, and heading in the opposite direction of the incoming team, they would be spared the bullets no doubt meant for them. He did not escape without harm, however. A head wound had dried blood just below his hair line on his face. The result of an unfortunate encounter with the one that caused this mess. *We should have just put a bullet in him*, he thought as he carefully poured himself a mixed drink, heavy in liquor and just enough juice to add a touch of flavor, and downed it quickly. The SUVs behind and in front of his limo keeping the pace moving at high speed. The jostling of the limo back and forth on the dirt-covered road was frustrating as he spilled his drink repeatedly before finishing it off and making a second. *No matter,* he thought, *they have all of the data that they need.* It was just a matter of getting it into the right hands. Even with the loss of his flagship compound, it was not his only route. He'd be back, and he'd wipe Cannon AFB from the face of the earth and one way or another, he'd claim his rightful place as the leader of the world. It was just a matter of time, as the convoy turned eastward, toward a new destination. As he watched the outline of the small concrete structure above the compound fade from view, the Praetor smiled.

The End

Acknowledgements

This ever-evolving story is only possible because of the three that I dedicate this book to. My mother Sandra and father Ken, and my step mother Dee. My mother with her unwavering strength, a single mother of four children. We never went hungry growing up, and what I learned from her more than anything is that we can handle it. We can handle whatever life throws our way. My father, a Navy veteran on the other hand taught me the importance of doing what needs to be done. As he said, "Take everything in life that you don't want to do, but need to. Take all of that shit, and make a shit sandwich and eat it." In other words, tackle all of the things that you don't want to do as early as possible, because after that it's done. My step mother Dee had been absolutely supportive through my teen years, helping to guide me through the war-zone that is high school. This story began with me hiding in my dark room, Linkin Park blaring through the headphones in my freshman year. It is these three amazing souls that led to this, and to ever upcoming story. Thank you three for teaching me things that even today I still am happy to learn.

Final Words

This book is part two of the Long Road Ahead series by Thomas Key. If you'd like to be kept in the loop about upcoming novels, or just want to support a new author, please see the links below. As always thank you for your support, and thank you for reading The Turning!

www.Thomaskeybooks.com

www.facebook.com/thomaskeybooks/

https://www.instagram.com/thomaskeybooks/

Made in the
USA
Monee, IL

15694377R00213